For Lee and my family,

BEWARE THE ILLS

By Patrick W. Marsh

Chapter One

The Hunt

I will never tell you my name. It's not important. It gives no specific view to my personality and character, not that there is much to observe. A name is simply a title, a label, a strand of living data to give you immediate worth in the chaos. It's worthless. Worth can only be earned. There is no need for anyone's full realization about me. I'm not allowed to be close to anything or anyone. I prefer it. I need to always be clear, always lucid. No room for error. Perfection's attractive, and so can being perfect. I must be able to kill with consistency and certainty, and ignore all distractions. Consistency always feels like perfection.

Nothing's more important.

It's snowing, like always. It snows every day in some random capacity on this island. I cannot consider it my island. I don't own the island. I don't have money. I've never owned money, but I know the island like something I own. I know almost every inch of it, from the dark of the Ill's tunnels in the grey stone mountains, to the cracks along the Shingles. I know the forest from its needled edges surrounding the shore, to the clearings near the river dividing this island.

Almost every inch, every snow-ridden inch, I have witnessed and known.

The island always stirs with a constant coldness. The wind blows in from the sea. The wind howls in from the mountains. The Ill's control the mountains bordering the ocean. Only one beach froths on the whole of the island. It has sharp and unwholesome white sand from the dark waves. I've watched this one shore countless times.

I try to forget it. I hate memorizing every little detail out of boredom.

The ocean roars under the wind. I can picture it now, the shore, the white brushing back at the water, throwing up warped shapes in wet bursts. I can't see the beach now. It doesn't matter, I know they're landing. New encroachers, new invaders, new outlanders, from some faraway country. I can faintly see their outlines through the trees. Blue and I have climbed high and deep into the velvet canopies. We are not in the highest tree of course, that would be ridiculous and stupid. They would spot us, especially Blue, and we would lose nearly all our allure. Surprise and legend, those are our most powerful attributes to killing. Without those two arrogances, we'd be just another pair of natural disasters.

I hear machines grinding. I hear men screaming over the west wind and flaking snow. The cold bites, and I breathe it. It stings wickedly today, it's so bitter. It draws my skin back in stiff lines along my white face. The cold began yesterday, and it normally breaks in the afternoon in some capacity or another. Mind you, it's always cold. This however, this winter has been the coldest in some time.

Blue growls behind me, he's getting restless. It's time to move, even he knows that maneuver. I breathe deeply and shake my face in the cold. There are more trespassers to kill, more to add to the graveyard, a timeless routine. I replay the image in my mind a few times to savor it. I smile.

We move.

We're falling. Blue drifts before me. He's heavy and bulky, not that it matters in a fall. When all this hunting began it would be one quick experience when I would fall. All objects would mesh together in a blurred image. Air would bite, green-needles would sing, and the weakest appendages of trees would be severed by my curled form. My armor would clap my shoulders on the landing, it would make me wince and blink my eyes. The pain doesn't happen anymore, too many calluses. Now I fall and time petrifies nicely. The trees are quiet. I can nearly see the faces within them smiling at me. I was never surprised to see them. They are living things after all. The faces come more often now than before, like I am always being watched by some hidden, tree-masked spook of the island.

The clouds still, sunlight stops also, all objects obey my descent. I land, nothing stirs, but the ground splits deep beneath my feet. Blue lands behind me, spinning his body around wildly in a hulking flourish. It's ridiculous, these flamboyant stunts. He takes joy in the strangest things. The quakes from his fall make the tree's thrash subtly and the ground echoes a hidden thunder for them to hear, ponder, and tremble.

We run.

Never stop, or at least rarely stop when moving in the forest. Whenever we fall we normally run, even if the forest yawns empty of marauders or Ill's. I tilt between the trees slightly as we dash. We stop and crouch down on the snowy carpet to hide. Consistent movement isn't always synonymous with progress. We dart again, or I dart, Blue is less nimble. If he falters and crushes a tree or brush of twigs, I'll cut his face so it'll bleed into his eyes. We can't give anything away, not a single thing.

We run faster.

The sea wind throttles back at us as we run. The snow whirls as we move—a convenient and masking flurry. The landing sounds are intensifying. We're getting close to the newest batch, the fresh round of marauders. We fall onto the snow knees first and crawl with our noses. No point in blowing the game. We slither past rocks and trees twisted with heavy green moss and spiked frost. I see forms silhouetted close to the hill overlooking the shore. The snow is covering us slightly as we crawl. It feels whimsical or polluted, like it's always better than us. My breath pushes a path through the flakes. Blue makes a low grumble behind me as we crawl. His form isn't suited for such low stalking.

I will cut him if he complains further though, don't think I won't.

I would always cut him above his eye when he was young and disobedient. The spot would always heal quickly according to his bodies systems. More importantly, blood would rush into his eye until it sealed. The wound was always more for annoyance than a physical pain. I haven't had to do that for quite some time. I scarcely remember how to do it in fact. I'd have to think hard before doing it.

We stop crawling.

I have found a place to observe them. A thick tree has been toppled from one of the cold storms, hewed right at its base in spectacular fashion. It still holds most of its big limbs on top, and below are hundreds of smaller cracked strands, which give us good cover in the crushed mass. I look out into the forest intently. The black stumps are smiling. Each tree's beams crawl up to the sky like old and mossy prayers. Their needles are a sick bright green and are covered in patches of fresh snow. The ground below them billows unevenly with mossy green growth and drifts of snow.

I can hear the sea far more clearly now. I picture their ships in my mind. They're covered in metal and wood, probably some lightweight metal suited to the stormy seas surrounding this island. No doubt a metal undiscovered in the Diamond Town. They don't spend any time looking for new things. They're too wrapped up in the old materials and beliefs, or that's what I'm guessing.

I haven't been there for years.

Most of the invaders come here with big, but still maneuverable ships. They know the combat will be on the island mainly. Seldom have I had to kill men on the deck of ship. I hate the sea, it surrounds everything so emphatically. The mountains on the north side of the island have a similar attitude. They're a consistent grey, a bleakness always lingering on the horizon. I imagine the Diamond Town should be happy with their presence, even though they house the Ills. The island's infested with the Ills. I don't mind slaughtering them and feeding them to the ground.

The sea next to the white sand sits black, hollow, and deep. It's so close from our hiding spot. The sea isn't lifeless, no, not from what I have seen. I still hate it, the dull roar of the waves, the spraying salt, the ridiculous black piling over and over again. It makes me sick. Still, in the sea there are things, in fact in the sea there are monstrous things. Monsters are there, many of them drifting deep in the dark. Occasionally, they wash up on the shore from time to time. They die of old age down there with nothing hunting them.

A peaceful, undisturbed death, then a rigorous float back up to land.

They're white as the snow these tentacle things. They have what seems like a hundred arms. Some arms are longer than others. If you were to stand them up from tentacle to tip they would be as high as the Diamond Town walls. A few of the arms have wide round ends with holes curling up into rings. I have seen these holes effortlessly rip the skin off man, much to their disappointment and dismay.

The skin, it came off like crumpled paper.

Their head's long, like a pyramid of sorts with a single eye in the middle. The eye wiggles like black marble, guided by a few glimmers of light darting back and forth. The eye makes me laugh. This wild behemoth circling the deep along the shore adorned with such a crazy eye looking in every direction, with such a large body—what a cruel joke.

When I trained in the waves I would swim out faraway from shore where the sea would slightly settle. I would stare down at them. I could see their long white bodies circling the blackness restlessly, until one would sense my vibrations and dart up towards me in a silvery flourish. It was very invigorating. I would then casually swim to the drop off close to the shore and walk onto land. They would burst through the water in a frothy spray and immediately try mounting the stones and shore. Their bodies are too awkward for life on land, their arms whirling wildly as they try to ascend the rocks in the shallows. I never stayed in too long after that however.

I have sat in the trees along the shore and watched the Ills who would fish for food in the shallows. They would wait for them with their long white arms hidden in the muck and mud along the rocks. They'd be slaughtered effortlessly and silently. Even for me, it was a hideous thing to observe and remember. I would not survive an encounter with them as much fun it would be to induce them.

I would not survive, not wrestling in the deep and dark.

No focus on that today, no focus on monsters in the deep sea. The invaders who have arrived must have repelled them. They are boarding the island unmolested and intact. The altercation between the invaders and sea monsters demonstrates competence. So many invasions do not reach the shore even. This is always a very disappointing and anti-climactic conclusion for Blue and I.

I must concentrate. I hate when separate nagging thoughts distract me at semi-pivotal moments in reality. Memory always crawls into ill-placed moments in my routines.

They're on the hill where the white sands arch away from the black broth. There are no paths to walk. I allow none, except for the ones the forest and wind have carved themselves. It would be disrespectful to eliminate them. Close to the shore, and just a little ways up the white hill I have placed a few corpses empty of all their tissue except a tiny amount in their chest. The corpses wear foreign armor, which shimmers with a lost gold. The armor looks quite alluring. I place it there to observe whether this batch of invaders will be distracted by some slight treasure, or stay focused on the goal.

It's necessary intelligence. The corpses also instill both wonder and certainty.

The corpse makes a certainty, a certainty all tales are true, and the wonder could be factual.

A white hand splits the forest on the white hill. The hand moves slightly erratic as it parts the green needles. It pushes and breaks the stems. The hand freezes at the sight of the corpse and retreat, like it needs to ask a question. He or she will not retreat long. Blue grumbles beside me. He starts stirring the snow with his giant hands. We've been holding too long for him in this position. The cold changes are getting harder on his joints. Nothing to be ashamed of, it's cold here, very cold.

The invader slowly shoves through the soft layer of trees with his armored side. He's white and withered. He has little to no hair on his face. That's an uncommon trait for most my visitors. He's clean shaven, edged, and blue eyed in his face. He looks straight ahead. I see the snow gleam off his eyes. He's blinking a lot, the flurries are disorienting him. He has a weapon in his right arm. The angle of his pose suggests extreme weight's being carried, but he's also relaxed slightly, which suggests experience balancing hefty weight.

These are enjoyable moments of discovery. This makes me excited to kill them.

Blue hums behind me. I jab him in the ribs with my elbow. Strangely, sometimes he sings to himself, though I am fairly certain he has never heard music before, at least before I attained him. The trees are moving. The air piles atop itself in snow. I want to be closer, but I resist. I'm becoming impatient as I get older. I'm completely patient for months then in solace of change I grow impatient.

This trait, this cancer, it will never desert me, never.

He's retrieving someone to examine the corpse I have left advantageously on the white hill. There are more of them now, all men, all white and old. They're all clean, thin, and organized. They have armor as well, but I can't describe it well enough through the trees and gusts. The wind stings my eyes when I stare too long. If they're adorned in heavy armor, I imagine they have not scouted the island, or are knowledgeable of its climate.

Why wouldn't they do research? I'm embarrassed for them.

I hear twigs breaking and footsteps. They've broken through the woods and I can see their armor. Their armor looks fancy, which doesn't guarantee it's effective. It's not heavy iron armor, but not light tin either, but a moderate plated shell. The plates won't protect them against my swings, not at all. They will be able to stomp around the forest well enough with them. An armorer somewhere did them justice. Curious to who designed mine. I never knew them. I only know it must have been a while ago.

Their armor covers their entire body except for their faces. The armor gleams a deep brown, like the trunks of the trees across the plains. The armor's plates are round and linked together with little brown rings. The helmet's narrow and pointed; almost pyramid like with a sharp point and no face mask. The cold will wear them thin there, like old living leather. It'll streamline the air right into their face. Glad someone else will get worn by the cold. A cloth hangs down on their ears to cut the wind. Smart, it's thin enough to block the sounds of war and the errant gusts of the wind.

They're looking at the corpse, turning it over all quizzically with their weapons, like children with some random dead animal. Why do humans in all new situations revert back to their adolescent awkwardness? I don't understand. It's delightful to watch from a far. I close my eyes and picture them without looking. The armor color blends well, very well. They might slip a few through my vantage points, they might.

The air smell's clean, very clean. The cold sterilizes everything I like to think. If the cold's anemic, then it's a very dirty island, especially with all the dead bodies and such. I stare through the snow a little bit harder. It's a crossbow, definitely a crossbow. It's grey and has a nice little cluster of gears in its innards where their hands are holding it. It look's heavy and obscene. It'll weigh them down on this island. It has multiple cords instead of just one. They're lined up in a way to making firing repetitive. Pretty clever, that's a new feature for the crossbow. They have a quiver of arrows leisurely strung on their belt to reload the contraption.

They have started to move in a horseshoe formation. They always move in one, some demented routine for every fresh batch of invaders. The taller men take the edges, hopefully to have enough line of fire, and not to hit the other snails. It's a smart enough tactic. They use the shore as a rearguard; well everything in front of them can be covered by their sights. They always do that too, the repetition feels beyond mindless.

The monsters in the deep are singing and moaning. Their songs hang lovely and eerie against the woods. I appreciate it beasts. The wind hits them from between the trees; it slows them slightly as they adjust. The lack of a path for them to walk along, forces them out of their formation. I'm not concerned. They will move slowly enough to me. I'm not concerned at all.

The absence of paths makes all invaders solitary, eventually.

I need to see all their weapons, not just those clumsy crossbows. This might be difficult judging by their body language as they roll in. Very cautious and very professional in their stances and marches, they're well trained. They've come for the Diamond town. I mean why else would they arrive? They always hear of the metropolis. The famous city built in the grey mountains, jammed and stocked with diamonds. I don't completely remember it. It's been quite some time since I have been out there. Riches, fame, jewels, gold, they come seeking all those useless things.

Death on a cold island might be the bleakest ray of reality to their lovely fantasies. These are already pathetic men.

I've set another corpse near the one they just passed. The body was even more decayed than the previous one. I keep them far away from the graveyard, which sits in the center of the forest, halfway to the Diamond Town. It's a woman. I've made sure the long hair has endured the decay. Barely anything else looks recognizable. She's a stew of dirt, bone, and strained tissue. They will see it. I don't remember when I killed her.

Back to the cold, back to the trap.

Next to the body nests a wire. The wire's attached to a tree I hollowed out a winter ago. Setting traps feels so pathetic and sloth-like. I hate it. I need the traps though, to judge their abilities, and their priorities. The wires will snag one of the men as they inspect the corpse. It will snare him and absorb the momentum of his struggle. It will carry him into the large hollowed tree adjacent to them. It's full of long hooks, pronged and clean. They're coated with a poison. The toxin causes madness, then death. The poison comes from the flowers on the edge of the valley before the mountains begin.

When they wilt it kills everything within a strong gust of wind. I melted the pollen and coated the hooks. Convulsions, madness, and then death in every creature they've been used on. Only I know the location of the flowers, no one else knows, not Blue, not even Haukter.

I wanted my weapon to be coated in the poison, but it's really unsporting, and not a quality I really want to my character. If enemies escape after I have cut them, then I hunt them down wounded. It prolongs the hunt, but at least it's honorable. Sometimes, the cold gets them after all that energy.

Sunken, unholy, limitless cold—I hate it.

The men are examining her. Their formation has unraveled from the woods. They look up to the forest, they will not see us, never has anyone seen us on the first gawk. Blue stirs behind me. I lightly slap him with my hand. He puts up his arms up when I do it to block me, but he only blocks me a little bit. He's smiling beneath the assault.

They can stop inspecting the corpse, nothing has changed. The two men are so similar, it's ridiculous. They bend down to touch her. That's unwise. They stop, abruptly, like they could hear my sarcasm. They prod her with their weapons, pigs with sticks, pigs with sticks.

Blue just keeps on growling behind me, he probably figures no one can hear him, but I can hear him. I prod him again. He was found in the grey mountains. His species looks similar to mine, to us humans, in fact we're disgustingly similar. They walk and lean like men. They have five fingers and two eyes. Their shoulders and arms swing and rip like men. But their bodies are covered in thick long white fur, thin at its ends but thick when it attaches to their skin. It's nearly impossible to pierce with metal or stone weapons. I know the marks though, the secret stabs—I know them.

I found Blue and his father in the grey mountains when I would wander the caves and tunnels looking for Ill's. I was deep in them, too far for the Ill's to even wander. I typically wouldn't go that far in, but I was bored, which happens often enough. I remember them very clearly. He and his father were at the end of the tunnel. I barely saw them. Their coats are a dusty grey blue that perfectly mixes in stone. The tunnel had no light except the orange beam bouncing off my torch. His father was growling at me and smashing the walls trying to scare me away. I had witnessed hideous things, it didn't frighten me. I was close to him. His paws and round claws were craving for my heart, for my skin. He charged me roaring and thrashing, even the mountain shook slightly to him.

It was quite the scene actually, rather intimidating.

I crouched down immediately. I couldn't hope to beat him up high, not a chance. I couldn't run since he would catch me easily. I couldn't do anything, but collide with him. I knew his back would be weak. Close to his spine sits a hidden spot there to split the steel fur, just a narrow enough spot for my sword tip. I let him hit me without sinking his claws in. I used his own momentum as I fell, and I threw him over my body with my feet. I followed him as he rolled along the ground stunned and confused. He probably hadn't known a man to take a hit and not die. I was on his back, my sword was through him and he was dead before he could roar. I had killed them before. Blue charged me then. He was still so small at that point. He was no threat, not even a hint of one. I smashed his head against the stone wall with my right hand. He was out before he could hit me.

I remember how his father's blood fell on the walls of the tunnel. It spread wild and wide in arcs, like the wings of insect.

I took him them out of the mountains. His father I couldn't leave, I needed the fur. When I started this I was given very little equipment. I needed something flexible to shelter myself with in a close and distant combat. I had relied on my reflexes too often, and any sentiment of luck attached to my physical skills was bound to wear out at some point. I restrained Blue against a huge tree that would take a small army to uproot. I needed fire for once so I built one. Against the orange light I began to skin Blue's father. He was passed out during this, even I am not clueless enough to allow him to witness this, and when he did wake up I would beat him senseless again. I did this until the morning when I released him. He was not happy to see me, and tried to flee.

I caught him and began the process again.

Now Blue hulks over me twice as big, and twice as strong. His face smiles round and exaggerated like a man, only he has round gnashing teeth and a big round nose. His face shines so blue, it matches the color of the sky with no snow, hence his namesake. His human hands are round and manlike with jagged nails that'll cut stone. His long white hair, which blankets him, falls down on his face covering his eyes. Only his smiling mouth can be seen. For so many years I had to watch him behind me. His strength and speed might be far superior to mine, but that's here, nor there when I know his weakness. Seeing his father's fur on me sustains his curiosity. It has been awhile since I have had to truly, non-playfully hit him. I don't even remember the last time I did. Even so, I cannot be completely alone in this endeavor, the others before me tried and they didn't last as long.

No one has lasted as long protecting the Diamond Town as I have, no one.

Now one invader just walks, the others have stopped and are watching him. They're suspicious, as they should be. The islands reputation must leer at them like an actual monster. Men file in on the hill between the trees. Maybe they have realized it's too easy; therefore, something must be wrong. They file in, and file in. It doesn't stop. Pretty soon the trunks of the trees are blotted out by their armor. I assume there are even more down on the ships. They wouldn't expose their whole number immediately. They're solemn as the snow falls, very solemn. Eight hundred eyes I count, eight hundred. They're all looking the same, all pale, all quiet, older men. Equal ranks, weapons, armor, all the same. Their lines are clumped and long, a symbol of intimidation.

One fool separate's from the metal herd. There is always that fool. A scout, a scout, I imagine he's a brave man, or else he would not have the position. He will hit the trap soon. They must be expecting some type of trap, some type of ploy. They must have received intelligence about it.

The purpose of the trap isn't some gory fixation or fetish for me. It's purely to identify how they will react when confronted with this bloody anomaly. They are all seasoned by their general appearance. Scars decorate most of their faces. So they will be calm when it occurs. But who will take command, who will try to remove the man from the hooks? That is the most important aspect of this whole grim surveillance. Blue would not wait for this observation, he would run howling in and kill them all, and he might be able to do it. As time goes by though, more and more invaders have tricks beneath their armor, devices for all means. They become more worrisome as time goes on.

I wish the wind would pick up and rattle the tree's a little more, and make one of them move forward. Blue's breathing very heavily. I can't hit an animal for breathing. I can't hit an animal for breathing.

The scout breaks his solemn stance and approaches slowly. His feet are following empty spots between the trees and branches. He trembles slightly. He knows their landing's too uneventful. He hits the trap. An eruption of snow screeches the air, immediately followed by a smashing of branches. He howls long and agonizing, it echoes across the timber. They don't move, they don't move. The wire's attached to some hewed trees scattered behind the edge of the forest. They mix with the other fallen tree's sitting like old giants across the island.

The wire whines and snaps as it pulls his ascent into the air. It's wrapped tightly around his lower leg, enough so a small stream of blood comes bubbling out as he spins. I need him to struggle so the tension opens the door. A few of the men chase after him running gingerly and cautiously. Someone along the line screams at them, but they continue to run. Blue starts to growl. I put my hand on his shoulder—he calms, it's too early for direct combat.

I need more information.

His body collides with the trunk. The hidden door on the front of the tree falls off in a wooden snap. Dried blood and rotted skin border the edges of it. The heavy door bounds off the tree and lands on one of the men crushing him. I laugh a little, I didn't expect that. The trap victim swings like a crying pendulum into the black hole of the tree. The angle of this spot isn't the best. I can't see him struggling anymore since the back of the tree faces me. The towering beam rattles and shivers under his struggle. The throaty scream thrashes loud and visceral, like an animal caged. The hooks I installed are large and curved. They're not meant to kill, sever or rip, even if the trapped man struggles, the hooks are too perfect. He will not be able to rip his skin off. I have never witnessed that type of audacity in trying to escape. It's painful though, the agony echoes across the snow and bounces across the trees.

I think they're use to this melody.

They've pulled the man out from below the door, he's bloody and broken. His legs were crushed and hanging out awkwardly. One of his arms was in front of him when it fell and it pushed a nice shot of bone through the skin below his elbow. It looks so obscene absent skin, like it really shouldn't be peaking out. They pull back to where the men have formed on the hill. They look so plain and boring standing on the hill. They look just like the trees.

I hate these boring comparisons to the landscape; unfortunately, I'm too used to these images. They mesh with reality over and over again like some demented visual concoction.

I am watching the ranks as the man screams. It does not disrupt my concentration. Not many sounds do anymore.

26

The brown rows of men spread out to where the trap shakes. They begin to part into a valley of armored grunts. A man parts the rows as he walks. He's very tall. I would only reach his shoulder standing on my toes. His face looks long and clean shaven, his eyes narrow, blue, and keen. His armor's deep black. He's marked, he's superior. The armor gleams the same as the other troops; round, plated, slightly worn for intimidation, and with no overtly exposed skin. Only his face hangs visible, with cloth or leather filling in each spot between the plates of armor. His helm curves the same as the others, only flat with a slight ridge to block the sunlight. His helm has more of a point to it on top, a commanding sign that could be seen above a clashing metal maelstrom.

Out of his appearance his hair would be the oddest commodity. It's long, feminine, reaching all the way down to his shoulders. He has earned a sliver of individuality. Sadly, his weapon's not on him or at least it's hidden beyond my eyes.

He walks slowly up to the tree. The victim screams, I'm sure he's stretching out his skin on the hooks. Every sharp movement by him blooms an elaborate synaptic explosion of pain. It's tedious. It's annoying. He examines the wire hidden in the snowy eves. He then examines the door to the trap I carved out, including the dried blood and fingernail marks along its round edge. The man who was crushed has been dragged away. He's dead of shock and twisted tissue. The tall man stares into the quivering tree. Snow falls off the eves as he thrashes wildly. He stares a long time at the man. He calmly grabs one of his cohort's crossbows and focuses it on the shivering tree. There is a quick burst of rattling, along with a hollow thudding sound. It sounds unnatural and foreign against the quiet snow. The back of the trees filled with points, they must fire arrows rapidly like I first thought. The metal the arrows are composed of must be lightweight for speed and strong enough to nearly pierce the timber. They won't be strong enough to pierce my cloak, but I am sure they fire with an elaborate frequency judging by the rattle.

They could knock me out if I stay still long enough. I will have to be cautious.

He was quick to conclude the event. I laugh quietly. His eyes dart upward and uphill towards our vantage point. He's observant. His eyes sit looking through the trees. Blue's gone under his emerald gaze. He can crawl across the entire island faster than I can run. His big upper body works well for crawling, but his legs are tiny. I use to laugh at them and trip him at full sprint.

I crawl to my right. I move silently and calmly. If they saw me now it wouldn't be over, but the mystique would be. There are some thicker needles on a cluster of trees just a little ways away. I crawl up a tree downwind from him. The snow blows hard at me again. The cold always bites more at heights. I brush it away from my eyebrows. The flakes make my forehead cold.

The brown ranks part as he walks back up the hill to the shore. An obscene amount of space holes out. He has complete command and fear. He walks to the hill and peaks down to the shore. A woman waits for him. She's watching him return. She has golden hair. It's long and tied in random spots with black bands. She's pale and narrow. Her face has quiet features in a soft chin and nose. I'm surprised she's wearing armor and especially that its pale white. The plated material's sickly looking just like her. Her piqued skin's exposed to the cold openly. No extra cloth or armor on her arms or neck. She wears a white cloak of sorts. It's long with some fur that hides her shoulders.

It's cold, even for me. She makes me feel colder.

She has a short curved sword tied to her belt. Someone who's stronger, in a brutish way, typically uses one of those. Giants and large brawlers who don't want to lose any momentum in a swing would use a short weapon. Not a woman typically. Funny, she has something attached to her belt. It emits a slow blue and green glow. She must have a hidden weapon. Haukter would appreciate it wherever he might be, close at hand no doubt. There's something in the center of her chest armor glowing a group of blue colors. Some sort of enhancement. Her belt has it too, and parts of her sides. It's blue and sapphire, and fused with laces of fine gold. She has eyes of the same distant green-blue. They're piercing and almost painful to focus on.

I have not tasted the blood of a woman for some time. This should be fun.

I am running away from their landing. Blue's already far ahead of me, he'll be heading towards the mountains to hunt Ills. No point in chasing him. We use to race each other across the forest and white hills, and he would always beat me. I can't beat his muscle and speed, but he doesn't know that completely. I'm still respected, yes, very respected. That hint of mystery assures my dominance.

The hidden mystery of how I killed his father.

We'll run towards the grey mountains at the end northern tip of the island. They stand over the teeming evergreen trees as dark black giants along the horizon. We will hunt Ills. They're not ready, the invaders, they're not ready for us to attack. It would be unseeingly to attack them when they're not at full capacity.

We'll freshen up first. We'll warm our fingers on the mountain side.

I can still hear the grinding and roaring of the gears. They must've brought some fancy contraptions with them, without a doubt. We'll pass the graveyard soon. The thousands of corpses, machines, and beasts stay frozen beneath the snow as we run—the vigil of dead cheering us on in their own solemn and quiet way.

Let them come, I've seen it all. They're all dead or hunched over, with the frost and flakes of snow singing to them. True art, true living sculptures, a grotesque mural to this islands livelihood. I won't stop now, only he and I go to the graveyard. Haukter, he's a strange one. He probably followed me there at some point, not sure when, but he's always lurking in my shadow. It's tedious.

We're through the forest now, and into the valley between the mountains and river. I'd find the Shingles if I veered right. I won't be near those walls anytime soon. I seldom return to it. It's completely empty, only past the wall and the narrow paths would I even find anyone.

The invaders are petty things. Petty things to come invade someplace they don't even know. They don't know where they are. They don't know who they really are. I have seen men and women of all shapes and sizes come through. I've seen all the machines and apparatuses stagger against the cold. I've witnessed hideous abominations take shape in front of my very eyes. Now they're frozen rot back there in the clearing. Let these fresh ones come, let them all come.

I will cut them all in two.

Chapter Two

The Ills

Worms. They look like worms. Veins I mean. Veins that are attached to severed limbs to be precise. They're outside the skin, leaking blood out of a round and dark tube. They have a meaty texture to their ends, and they glisten with fresh exposure. You notice how intricate the body works even when you've been doing this like I have.

Even when it's an Ill, not a human, you still notice things.

When I killed this particular Ill these severed veins belonged to, he wiggled his arms in the air as I pinned him down with my knee. He squirmed. I cut off his arms. I paused just long enough for his mind to catch up with the situation. He doesn't realize right away the blood violently spilling out belongs to him. Actually, Ill-blood resembles dirt in color, but in a liquid form.

He died of shock almost immediately after he came to grips with his situation.

I'm standing over his corpse. We're on the edge of the mountains. We ambushed the Ills as they walked in the open along the cliffy-face of a lesser peak. The sky brews clouds towards the shore, with smoky breaks where the sunlight casually peaks through.

The sun's never bothered the cold here. Nothing on this island deters the cold.

I can't help but think of that fresh crop of trespassers on the western shore. I imagine the trap will slow their reconnaissance. There are no more traps however, just the one. Traps in the end are ineffective. Invaders can adapt to them quickly. They've seen traps before. They've got experience with them. They've made that clear with their weathered expressions. I always give them a half day to get their strategies together, to build all their best violence for me.

I want them to be at their best, that's not selfish of me.

The grey cliffs we're sitting on had been used by the Ills to put together a war party. The cliffs across the mountains are smooth from their little running feet. The landscape forever altered by them.

It vexes me with a strange terrain based jealousy.

I throw the Ill I killed onto his stomach. His face sits in a pool of his own blood. The rest of the Ills are blocked from the path leading back into the mountains tunnels. Their backs are against the edge of the cliff. Blue has pinned them there cleverly. They'd have to rush him to get back into the mountains mazes. We'd never find them in there, they'd have the advantage. They know those tunnels like rats. They have every nook and cranny memorized.

Blue's brawny arms are opened wide and menacingly. The span of his arms equals nearly three of me. He's showing them his nails too. They're blue and hard as stone. I'm sure the Ills know all about them. We've occasionally had to let a few live from our skirmishes. We need to preserve the intimidation and legend. Essential, it's flawlessly essential.

Blue twitches eagerly. He may not begin yet. We must preserve the moment.

No snow currently, but the air has a whirling cloudiness about it. The forest has a clear and lucid gleam. The snowy patches below the trees make their needles glow and shimmer. The Ills are firing arrows at Blue. They're crude black arrows with uneven points and feathers. This makes them uneven and unbalanced. Blue covers his face with one massive paw. He laughs at the Ills in his strange animal giggle. They're almost roars, but with a high quivering to them.

The Ills start to hiss and scream like walking-snakes. They're such vile creatures. They're shorter than men because their backs are hunched and riddled with lumpy deformities. Their form brewed from the tunnels and narrow halls they've lived in for centuries. Being bent down beneath a mountain your entire life would be irritating. Their skin glows a dark green like the needles in the forest. They're covered in blemishes and scars. They're very strong, stronger than men and sometimes faster. The Ill's lack intelligence however, and cannot conceive strategies or plans.

They're unable, and unfit for war games.

Their faces have larger eyes than men, but similar colors and centers. They have little hair, and their nose and teeth are exaggerated and shriveled. They wear worn and rusty armor that looks more brown than silver. The armor hangs tattered and worn from rubbing against the mountain walls. They always look random and bedraggled, no matter if we've just ambushed them or watched them from afar.

Watching them move around feels exhausting, they're clumsy and loud. If they had a hint of a mind behind their movements, then they might be dangerous.

There are thousands of them in these mountains. We've been killing them for as long as I can remember. It has never changed. I've never really noticed their population to be really hurt by it either.

I like this consistency though, it's good.

I don't know how many dance in front of us, but there all shapes and sizes. They're crying and wailing for help in chattering hisses. The cries are loud and irritating. They echo across the valley and into the trees. I'm sure they'll be heard, but it'll be too late at that point.

Blue drools for them. It freezes on the long hair beneath his chin into strange hairy icicles. I laugh at them. When Blue kills them, he rips off their arms at the shoulders and squeezes the blood out of their body. Eventually, they'll be dry and twisted like crusts of old bread. Blue also likes to crush them between his paws, until they're unrecognizable bloody green pieces of pulp. By the time he's done, they'll look like old green pieces of mud all twisted and misplaced.

The Ill's hissing and high-crying suddenly stops and they rush us in a stampede of rattling metal.

Blue swings back and forth at them as they rush. Each finger looks close to half the size of their torso. They look like little children in comparison to them, it's wonderfully obscene. Blue slashes wildly. They scream, and jab their black spears and swords in between swipes and rips. No effect, his hide deflects any of the rusty stabs actually landing on him. Blue leisurely collapses on them howling, or maybe even laughing. Blue grabs the first Ill and crushes it beneath one of his massive feet. It pops and cracks against the grey stone, while black blood leaks out in steamy black streaks. Blue crushes the Ill almost flat. He needs proper balance right now.

You always need proper balance.

More arrows fly now from the back of the trapped line. Blue raises his arms again to shield his face. He brushes them aside in mid-air in leathery black bundles. Two Ills break from the motley pack and stab for his arm pits where his iron-hide clusters weaker. They jab and stab incessantly along with screaming. Blue lifts up the corpse beneath his left foot, which is more like another hand, and throws it into the two charging Ills. The thud of meat on meat echoes and they fall down dead from the impact. Blue grabs one of their still bodies and wildly charges deeper into the swarm. The white-jaw has gotten him, he going to be out of control soon. He'll go into these rages where he can't control himself, his jaws become white along with his gums. The Ills, surprisingly, knew he would fall into this bloodlust. They immediately coordinate their assault. They fire arrows at his head and stab at him from below.

It's a little disheartening to see Blue so unorganized in the midst of his unchecked rage.

I run towards the cliff wall behind the melee. I jump onto the wall and bounce into the air. A few arrows rattle behind me as they strike the rock. Nice try. I'm very high. High enough for the wind curving off the mountains to catch my cloak and whip it wildly. I feel like I'm not a part of anything when I jump, not a single thing. I look below to the grey rock. I find my feet, and judge the width. My sword's out before I even hit the ground. When my feet hit I cleave two Ills in half at the waist. Blood funnels out in black geysers from the empty gashes above their waists. It smells like vinegar in the cold air.

I'm literally surrounded by Ills.

I contort my body, stick out my sword blade and swing in full circle. They scream high and low in their throats, a bizarre mixture of gurgling howls and muscle. The spraying blood drowns out the whistling, it's nice. I open my eyes to a dark black circle of severed body parts and sliced armor. I walk closer to the mountain side. I isolate one Ill and swing at it with my long sword. The Ill manages to parry my attack with its curved rusty blade. I grab the antique blade with my left hand and pull it close. I smile and slide the back of his blade against his throat diagonally in a deep gash. The Ill's quite beastly; it's been possibly bred in the belly of the mountains for the sole purpose to kill me. Another large Ill, with a scarred green face and spiked armor, charges me in a frustrated roar. I trip the Ill with my left foot as he clumsily swings a large black axe. The Ill falls forward surprised. I rip his round black throat out with my left hand as he falls. I quickly throw the black oily ball at the small cluster of remaining Ills. They cry at the sight of the big Ill dead and limp on the ground.

I smile, this is fun.

I begin to kill them one by one in terrible ways. For most of the Ill's, despite their varying sizes, I slit open their stomachs with the point of my sword. They always cry for help. Other Ills, I crush my hilt squarely into their chests so they inhale blood until they die in a hideous choking fit. We follow a criterion for all this, a true curriculum. Each method I use to kill the Ills must have long lasting psychological damage on the others. If an Ill escapes—they're too damaged to relate this encounter, or attack again.

Blue has picked off the stranglers from my clash one by one. He has begun to feed on them.

I can hear the bones crunching like small uneven rocks. I hear the skin stretching like old wood bending under the cold air.

It's quite a collage of sounds.

One Ill has escaped the feeding frenzy. I follow it towards the edge of cliff where it's backpedaling with fear. It's small, a child of sorts in their species. Why did they bring along something so small, something so young? Why? When I trained Blue he was never this small. People are so irresponsible when it comes to raising youth.

I spared a child once.

He survived the woods, the Ills, and now he stalks me ardently day and night. I will not show that courtesy again.

I hear Blue in the background drinking the blood ravenously, his throat muscles are contracting loudly in muscular claps. I grab the young Ill by the throat. A large stain grows on his torn grey pants. He's soiled himself. I look at him closely. He's very human looking this one, just the green skin to him—but nothing else hideous. I'm a little disappointed. I want them to look monstrous. I drop him off the mountain in a quick release of my hand. I watch him spin and thrash as the empty air surrounds him. He will be dead from panic before he realizes the rocks.

I can give him that.

More drinking, Blue has almost run through his whole supply of Ills. Blue's grey coat is draped in dark blood. A pile of squeezed corpses sits silently behind him. They're twisted and contorted, leathery and smooth, and absent all their blood. They look like old vegetables left out in the sun. The wind bustles up, the clouds have returned and the snow has started again. There are few Ills left alive. They wanted to escape but they were in shock, and now are begging on the ground. I leave them to Blue. I will leave the mountains to my pool. It's not far from this mountainside.

The pool quivers small and cozy. It's close enough to the graveyard to dissuade any unwanted visitors. I can almost always use the pool in peace. Only one comes to watch me there.

He's the one I spared.

I'm ready to leap from the cliff down into the needles of the forest. I will fall uninterrupted until I reach the trees, then I will ride their soft limbs down in small falls. I'm about to leap, but one of the Ills in Blue's paw begins to scream words.

There are words in my tongue.

He's an older Ill, with black ragged armor and a long beak nose. His eyes are nearly swollen shut with blemishes.

I stop. I'm not sure why.

"Stop, stop, no more, no more," the Ill yells in a shriek laden voice.

Blue growls a retort in some lost language.

"We don't need to war anymore. We have a prince who will be king soon," he screams shaking his hideous head.

The Ill stops thrashing at my silence and stares at me, memorizing my every detail. Should he live, he would tell those details, many details about me.

"He is not like us. He walks tall, his back is not bent, and his face is not scarred like mine," he screams.

I don't look at him as he speaks.

The Ill begins to laugh wickedly. Blue starts to crush him.

"He'll end the war, but I fear you won't allow that-" he gasps with his trembling green throat. His eyes roll back as Blue continues to squeeze him. He points at me. His arms come off, and the Ills veins jolt through its green skin lazily, hanging limp and flaccid like dark red ribbon.

Still staring, the Ill's still staring at me. I've got nothing to say.

The Ill starts howling; even more now that he's realized the last one's left. He's dead in a few moments thanks to Blue. I look at Blue drinking the dark blood. The liquid looks hot trickling off his maw. I can tell in his blue steel eyes he's wondering, why did I listen to this Ill?

I fall off the mountain side.

The mountains are only a continuous hue inching by me as I fall into the forest. There are cracks and traces to it, an uneven ocean of stone. I tilt my weight as I glide close to it. I jab my sword into one of the dark long veins. The silver metal grinds and sparks for a few moments, then stops. The pain feels good. I swing around with my left arm and flip onto the edge of my sword. I balance myself on the hilt and stand up. More clouds, more ashen clouds crawling across the olive tips of the forest. The frost dries out the skin beneath my eyes and nose. Tedious, the cold, it's always around. I know every detail to it, every long and arduous detail. The wind kicks up wildly. I use my cloak to block some of it.

Will Haukter be there today?

He won't be close enough for me to hear him, but he'll be close enough to watch me. I know he doesn't actually watch what I am doing, he simply wants me to know of his presence or he's around.

An ambitious undertaking, I admire the tenacity.

He won't fight me though, not till the odds are weighted in his favor. He's no physical match for me outright, but he's spent nearly all the living years of his young life hunting me in his mind's eye. Until newfound confidence for Haukter occurs, I will still go to my little silver pool.

I run full speed into the woods. The air's brisk, sharp, and omnipresent. I'll reach the pool before the next set of snowflakes begins. That's good, I hate seeing their little delicate designs melt on my shoulders. I close my eyes as I run. I can feel the air buckle and break as I dash through the forest. I reach a small hill. I can feel the incline in my feet and legs. I open up my eyes slowly.

That was fast, I'm already here, how sickeningly easy.

The pool sits inside the graveyard, adjacent to a clearing in the center of the forest. The pool curdles small and isolated. The pool's bank isn't littered with miscellaneous pieces of armor, body parts, or war machines. I wouldn't allow it to be tainted by these sullied remnants of invaders. Blue does not come here, nor do the Ills. I would feel them in the trees and hunt them, and I'd slit their ugly green throats.

A few tall trees surround the pool, dropping faint shadows over the water. The edge of the pool has a layer of round silver rocks, which are set very neatly and symmetrical around the clear water. I wonder if it was meant for me, or the other men before me?

The wind barely moves, even with just the few trees bordering it. The unknown forces in all their unseen glory are even timid of this location. The forest has an air of slaughter to it, everything senses it.

The pool's very shallow near its edges, but the closer you get to its center the deeper it grows. I like to dive down there and look at the round flawless stones at the bottom. There are things etched there, pictures, or shapes, or something. It could even be writing, names possibly of men like me before they were forgotten in all the killing. I can dive down my full length to this secret deep spot. The rest of the water comes up only to my waste in depth.

The water trembles quiet and still, truly tranquil, truly tranquil.

I'm covered in blood. The liquid has a dark and oily texture to it. In combat, it's impossible for it not to splatter it everywhere. The release of liquid encapsulated in the body truly has physics all to its own. The cloak of Blue's Father looks grey, almost silver. It aged without the being inside of it. The cloak covers my left shoulder. I need to have it separate and flexible, to have it move independently against missiles or arrows. It needs to be a living shield in all situations.

Nothing can pierce the Untaro's fur, no weapon anywhere.

I drop it in the pool. It gets heavy, and spreads dark red and black constellations atop the water. Beneath the pool jets warm water in a steady flow up from the bottom. The spring stops the water from freezing over. Only the big river in the center of the island, and this pool retain any surface movement in this cold. I can feel it on my feet when I go in. It makes my toes curl and reminds me of someplace else. I don't know where.

I throw the fur on top of the snow to dry, and start to remove my armor. The armor's black like sea water. In front sits a flat and round chest plate, which bears random straight lines intersecting in diamond-shaped designs. I've never know their origin. I've wondered about it. The same pattern curls out on my right shoulder where the armor stretches out into a black point. When I run through crowds of invaders, I use the sharp edge of the point to cut at eye or throat level.

I am not very tall. I would say average to whatever shows up on this island. I've killed some tall things though, height's an illusion.

On my left shoulder where my cloak normally sits, use to be another spike, but I removed it because the cloak would get hung up on it. The armor has a nice pure black color. It's simple and blends in night. After I remove the chest plate and back plate, I have one piece left on my left arm. From first glance it'd be essentially a wrist guard, but it's not just that. You have to multitask often out in the forest. My wrist guard has a small hook that curves out slightly. Essentially, I use it the hooked grove to catch blades in when my right arm's busy. I also use it to catch skin and stretch flesh. It's been a while since I've had to utilize it. I remove it and lay it on the rocks, not far though, not far at all in case I need it.

I wear a long sleeved garb beneath my armor, it's thick and heavy. The black fabric absorbs the cold well. It covers my neck. I found a whole pile of them in the Shingles within the secret room. Some of them are worn out or blood-ridden. I inspect the hook from my left arm, and it's still sharp. The elements haven't dulled it at all. I've caught the heaviest weapons imaginable in it, and not a splinter of steel or wood has crawled into my skin. I don't need to sharpen it, though I would like to, it's a very engrossing task. I'll wait for another time. I've got a lot to think about after all.

I am holding it now, my sword, my other arm, or anything else that bears relevance to a limb. My sword has my mind and my body in one pure action. The sword wasn't mine by chance. It was atop a mound of snow outside the room in the Shingles. The Shingles stand as the last line of defense for the Diamond Town. Since everything began on this miserable island with the invaders, they've thrown up walls year after year until us guardians came into being. Therefore, a huge line of poorly built grey walls have sunken in and moved uneven across these blood epochs. Most of the walls are a quarter of a mountain high or smaller. There are no gates or entrances. The walls make a crooked line of uneven squares. Apparently, they look like square shingles of the roofs in the city.

I don't remember the city very well, but apparently they're like that.

The sword spreads two of my arms spans. It's a longer sword than most would use. It's not curved or thick in the blade. It's built more narrow or needle-like, with a tip that has a small point and two recognizable edges. Two tips are important for stabbing. The armor invaders use in the forest typically has thickness at vital areas, but never completely linked—leaving room to puncture. The hilt of the sword hangs black and straight. The wings of it are silver and square. They're wider for balance when you swing it. They can also puncture and stab if need be. The handle has padded lines for gripping. It's long enough to grip it with two hands, but I rarely have to use two. Below the handle sits a white, yet round piece of metal with an etched circle that means something. I don't know what. The little metal teardrop adds a little weight for more balance.

I keep the sword in a sheath strapped to my back. My armor has a built in a spot for the scarab to lock into my armor. The scarab looks black and curved, and heavy with simplicity. The hilt of my sword always menaces above my right shoulder; that is the perfect place to put it. Before, I had my sword strapped to my belt, but that would disrupt my balance when I would run. It got tedious so I moved it to my back. Apparently those before me had the same problem. With the sword being on my back, my right hand can get grab the handle fast and I need less time to pull the blade out.

The sheath doubles as a secret weapon. It's heavy, yet easy to throw. It would have enough force to cave someone's chest in, therefore crushing their heart. I've never used it in the height of combat; it has never been needed as thus. Still, I hope that point occurs someday. It's a last resort, a last resort.

Haukter uses all hidden weapons, whenever I've reversed roles and watched him in the forest I can never tell what types of weapon he carries. But still torture, very effective, very effective.

I have very little possessions, no need, and no need. My slacks are heavy black cloth and my boots are durable and narrow. The choice of the color black for my apparel was due to the surrounding environment of trunks, braches, and trees. I'm part of that solemn army, camouflaging me quietly.

I appreciate the paranoid trees. I do. I do.

I look at myself in the clear reflection of the pool. I'm a pale sight. I have long arms, a long torso, and shorter legs. Every vein and white muscle has been developed, but not overtly so that I can't be flexible. Being able to twist around my sword adequately, functions better than chopping through limbs with every strike. Every second I don't watch the forest I spend training, and exercising. For me, being prepared remains essential for survival. It grows tedious after a while, but to go without it would be like denying air to breathe. Every second I don't spend hunting, killing, or even stalking—I need to exercise. I can't stress the routine enough, the upkeep's beyond essential.

I must remain strong because Haukter trains also, he trains and prepares for me.

I push on the rocks and feel the water flutter beneath my feet. The water sings so clear, so lucid and untainted by obstacles. I have to wash off every speck of the Ills blood from me. No blood must remain, no pore left clogged or clustered. I always keep my face clean shaven. It restores my humanity after everything. My face isn't elusive or original, just round, thin, and white. My hair's matted, curly, and slightly long. When it gets long enough and can hang into my eyes I cut it off with my sword. My face is still thin, unblemished and pale. I do not look at myself often, rarely ever. My muscles are still not as sinewy as they were before. I see the veins less, the muscles less defined.

The water turns cold, I have soaked up too much of the heat, if that's even possible. I dive down beneath the water and close my eyes. My hair floats to the surface. I can nearly feel the biting wind through its tips. If the water were steel, it would easily pierce me.

I am no inhuman, no half-monster, or spirit man. I am no embattled curse, phantom, or ancient creature. It has never been my role to be a complete monster. I am completely man, no extensions, no spells, and no hallowed artifact to give me power. I've see all these enhancements though, and I've slaughtered them all. I was given this role long ago. It would not seem consistent or clean to change now and cheat within my methods.

It would be unsporting to rely on mysticism.

Sleep happens when it cannot be denied any longer. When I need to sleep, I run as fast as I can to a hidden place in the Shingles. I run zigzag and random across the forest till in my bones I feel comfortable enough to sprint towards my actual sleeping place. None can find me. None can match my running across the white hills and between the black trees, not even Haukter. The hidden place sneaks between two of the leaning squares of an old grey wall in the center of the Shingles. It's below the towering stones and hidden amongst the maze-like walkways. You find it by a crack in the wall, which looks like a black vein running into the ground. Where the crack meets the ground stands a hidden stone door, which swings out on metal hinges. The door was built long and low to the ground. It's perfectly hidden, only those who know where it is would be able to find it. Inside waits a small stone compartment, just big enough for a full grown man to sleep.

I was drawn there when I was young.

My first night after they threw me from the wall, I was too afraid to wander out from the Shingles. Walking in-between the massive tilting squares I found an orange light. There was a black torch stuck into the crack above the portal. The door took me a while to find in the gloom. I couldn't figure out the reason for the torch at first, and I wasn't able to find the door until morning. I remember putting my little hands beneath the door and grimacing when the stone would scratch my hands open in faint bloody streaks. The door was heavy—it took a while to pull it open. When I finally did get it open, I remember being strangely excited despite being thrown to the wild. Inside was the armor, and clothing. It was all prepared for me.

Back to the water, back to the water. I am nearly finished in the water. Every scrap of blood must be removed—every speck. The Ills blood feels corrupt, and monstrous. It would poison me if it remained stagnant on my skin. The armor will not rust to their blood. It's made out of a hidden ore from deep inside the mountains. They call it something special, but I can't remember it. The armor blocks everything that's been thrown at me. There has been quite a collection. My sword was made of the same material as well. Normally, it can cut through everything, not in one strike but if I hack over and over again. The sword has never lost its edge, never.

I put my armor back on—my body has been cleansed. The cold eats away all the other hidden decays. I hate the sultry stink of the Ill's blood, it follows me endlessly. I get dressed and approach the woods.

I run.

More snow falls, it's picking up under the white clouds. I've memorized every pattern of it, it's very redundant. The white, the cloud, all of that detail, it's very repetitive.

I keep running. I don't really keep track of where I go or where I am.

Night falls suddenly. At the interior edge of the Shingles where people of the Diamond Town still roam around occasionally, they will light the torches. The torches are elaborate trees of metal and wood that sit behind the Shingles. There are literally hundreds of them. Each one looks like a cube of ice melted into a perfect square. They are lit inside with a hidden fuel, which only the city knows about. They throw random beams of orange light into the forest and usually cover the sky in a sickly faint orange. I always assumed they were for me.

It would be a little heartbreaking to find out differently.

I'm running still, running fast not to be attacked and not to be followed. I am heading back towards the graveyard. It is quite the display.

Haukter follows me.

He's following me, trying to keep pace. He will keep his distance. He is most certainly not ready for direct confrontation. Physically, he might finally be my equal, but he can't take that chance. Whenever he truly confronts me, he will only have that one confrontation. If I were him, I would wait till I am truly distracted. It might be his only chance.

There is some unique chaos out there, it could happen.

I am nearly there, back to the graveyard. The snow beneath my feet has a hint of the torches dull orange, and the black night makes everything glow a little bit more than usual. The trees are dark, man-like; there are faces in them I swear.

I have found them glooming in the dark—the shapes of the walking machines loom largely in the dimness. Corpses spread at their trunks and feet. They are hard to see even with the beams of orange light. The orange light usually gets caught in the needles high up in the trees. The illumination has a hard time falling down to my vision. The shapes of the machines are all types, curved, blocked, rigid, and jagged. Every type of machine imaginable stands silent and unmoving. Machines that roll on wide wheels, walk on legs, or walk on four legs. Machines that are platted, chain mailed, or of solid wood. A few machines are absent the armor they arrived in and have a network of gears and rods exposed. They've rusted and decayed since their arrival. They're just like the outer armor of the other machines. I can't remember all the machines. I think some may even be before my time in the woods.

For all the glory and education brewing in the men and women behind these machines, they are pretty flimsy in comparison to the elements. Even ostentatious metal can still bleed, starve, and sicken. These shells are only for vanity, confidence, and a little extra feeling when walking the woods of legends and hidden monsters.

I do respect the efforts of the machines, but they wear and rust in the cold, till they turn into one mangled heap, like a freshly born animal.

Machines may be littered far and wide, but the skeletons poking and protruding with skins of frost and snow truly create my desired ambiance. Invaders bring beasts with them from all the corners of the world. There are horses of sorts, roaring cats with thick manes, reptiles that breathe bits of fire, and man-like creatures strong and bloodthirsty, but lacking any sort of intelligence. Other monsters are summoned from smoke and mirrors placed on the ground. But still, all these beasts turn to skeletons in the islands center. Blue is different to me, somehow, he's not an animal anymore.

I hear the bending of snow and breaking of tree roots.

It's him, Haukter, watching me from the edge of the dark trees. He's seemingly blending into the woods as he stalks.

Impressive, it's very impressive.

I call him Haukter, it's a name I remember from when I was small. He came here many years ago, I cannot remember when exactly. They were outlanders, invading this island, a whole long trail of them. They were dressed in long and wide clothing that almost looked like sand. It covered their entire body save their eyes. The winter killed most of them within the first few days. I killed the others. When I killed the last invader in their tent, it was a woman who was freezing and delusional. There was a small form by the last bit of their flickering firelight. She had hidden in the tent—a little boy not past the age of seven or six. He was beneath a pile of frost covered animal furs and hides.

So ridiculous, it is so ridiculous to bring a child along a war path.

Why bring them? It was ridiculous, I couldn't kill him. I knew the winter would, I knew it. The winter kills almost everything I miss. It's quite my phantom partner.

Haukter survived. He survived the forest, the Ills, the winter. He has followed me here to watch, to observe. He's a young man now, in his prime. He typically wears layers and layers of animal hides and cloths over himself. They hang down in baggy rolls, so you can't actually see his form.

They're black and brown in random patterns of fur. He wears a thick bulky hood over most of his face except for his eyes. They're the only thing left uncovered. His eyes are green-blue still, like they were by the flickering fire long ago. He has antlers and feathers hanging from his hood. There's more to him, but the torches glow are weak here, not enough detail.

He has weapons, hidden weapons. He wouldn't wander the forest unarmed and exposed. I sense them with hidden eyes. They're for me, and only for me I hope.

I would be insulted if his savage existence was not going to be released upon me.

I hear something on the shore, he has heard it to. It sounds like metal throbbing against empty air. It's a large machine rattling. It's large enough to echo from the shore with metallic clarity. The sound's getting louder and clearer almost ascending into the clouds and falling snow. A flying machine, yes, it has to be. It'll launch in the daytime—they would be fools to send it out at night. They must be testing it, getting a feel for the high air currents, and the winds coming off the mountain. It will be a tricky flight for them.

It's been a while since I've had to take down an airship.

The moon spreads out just beyond the thick clouds. Blue beams hang between the flakes and dark lumbering shapes. I'm sitting on the skeleton of some beast killed long ago. It's huge, curved, and has three huge horns across its skull. I'm sitting on its ribs, their curved and massive, bigger than Blue even. My weight makes them creak and groan. What a sky, stars spread out in endless thin stabs of light.

Haukter is gone, the sound drove him away. An airship, exciting, it's been very a long time.

Chapter Three
The Airship

I'm running. Blue sprints far behind me panting and grunting frost clouds. He's judging the distance from the ground to the flying machine. The space looms a bit harder for him to calculate. The gap of empty air yawns long and daunting. I have a few reservations about it myself.

I always do when storming an airship.

The morning air bites clear, white, and repetitive. A paper-thin cover of white clouds hangs on the sun, dropping a weird gloom across the trees and hills. I was awake all night waiting for the airship to crest over the trees from the shore. Most airships are awkward looking things bumbling slowly and lazily like an oversized insect. This contraption glides quite fast, easily the fastest I've ever stalked before.

The metal bug has the speed to reach the Shingles in a few hours. It took the invaders all morning to balance it in the air. The night was too dark for me to see it in detail, and the torch light falls limp and worthless by the time it reaches the shore. All I could see was them using the trees as towers to balance it. There were long coiled lines connected from the airship to the ground.

Still running, we'll have only one moment to try this maneuver. The trees are a blur, the constant colors smear, and the cold becomes just another nagging thought.

This is why I love to run.

The island bubbles with hills through the shore till the mountains. Before the mountains, a green and white valley blooms up like a sore. In the valley there are flowers that when they bud and wilt in the cold, they'll kill everything. Haukter uses them; specifically, they are the source of his disgustingly devious poison.

I can't think about him right now. The hills, I must time them.

Focus, you always must focus. We'll use the hills in all their white, endless glory to leap off and cling to the base of the gliding machine. Haukter's following, he's always there. I know it. He's keeping his distance. Doesn't he have anything better and more productive to do with his time? He would never try to confront me with Blue present. Even that would be too much for him. Haukter's permanently powered by a well-developed fuel of revenge; therefore, having Blue present serves as a ferocious and lovable insurance policy.

Finally, a white break opens among the ceiling of trees. The sky peers through cloudy and white to reveal the thundering airship. It's wide, round, and somewhat flat like a fish's belly. A nude, petrified woman with long hair and long limbs has been etched into the metal on the point of the ship. It looks ridiculous. The ship's armored in black steel, and laced with strings of gold bars lining across its sides. The gold gleams flawless and shining in the dull white light. It must be a very high quality.

They would be more likely to survive this without a sense of vanity.

There are two spinning contraptions at the end of the wide deck. They look like a bird's wing absent the feathers, spinning in black metal circles. That awkward looking thing must give the ship flight. They hum lazily as they pass over the tree tips. They're taking their time to the Diamond Town.

They don't feel threatened yet.

Blue and I are looking for our window to leap. The hills will give it to us, but only for a moment. Only a few seconds will be needed.

The airship continues to thunder idly. The flapping metallic sound echoes through the canopy. The lethargic and secretly strenuous hum from the machine's twirling engines confirms this machine's not truly meant not to fly. It has some sort of leathery bubble-skin above its main deck, which captures air and sustains its weight. The skin's coated in some sort of thin metal. It's connected to the rails with round black chains. Inside must be some sort of cabin or structure to house the grunts. I have seen it in other airships. I usually cut the belly so they all spill out.

Typically, it's red and dribbling disarray.

There are three large white hills before us, and at the third peak I will reach the needed velocity. At that time I will jump and use a tree at the base of the hill as some sort of leaping board. When I break the ceiling of the trees, the bottom of the airship will nearly be within my reach. I will be able to stab the ship with my sword and gain a foothold. The maneuver has happened before and I am confident in its consistency. I'm looking forward to the view above the trees. The spectacle's rare in comparison to our typical vantage points. The view of the mountains and the Shingles from afar, like an old lost world riddled with stone giants.

The twist and turn through the empty air above the trees will be very invigorating. I like the idea of no physical structure holding me in the air.

Blue's now keeping pace perfectly, he knows the moment of our maneuver draws near. His form, though bulky and huge, can move easily between the trees and needles. The petal thin snow falls, and sticks to my hair in melting bubbles. Still, I'm not sweating. Blue's lucky, his coat deflects the snow and keeps him eternally dry. He's a lucky beast. He will attack after I make the airship land. He can leap higher than me, and I will alter the course of the airship back towards the trees so he can engage the force after it has completely appeared. His iron fur's ideal for close combat, and on the deck of the airship you'll need good balance and a calm head.

He has neither and always, sometimes.

The second white hill rolls close, the window's coming, the window's coming. I will not allow any mistakes, none. My weapons are ready, my cloak, my armor, and my gauntlet. All are sharp, ready, and balanced. The trees are breaking before us now. We no longer care about dodging them. This all-encompassing feeling, it prepares you, and boosts the hidden fire in your chest.

Exciting, what machines will they have? What weapons, besides those clunky crossbows?

I'm running at top speed now. Blue starts panting again behind me, he puts his hands on my waist and we run in unison, it's difficult, but it can be done. We reach the top of the hill and we both leap into the air. Everything stands still slightly, this was a big leap. Blue pulls me back towards him, and leaps onto the trunk of a tree on the downward slope of the hill. He shakes and trembles in the air. Is it fear, or excitement? Is there a difference?

He bounces us up past the trees.

The airship buzzes directly overhead. I can see the bolts and metal lines along the bottom of the ship. I can see the statues lash-heavy eyelids on the port bow. The airship hums drolly, like it was completely unimpressed by our aerial maneuvers. Blue spins and launches me into the air with all this strength. I'm literally thrown across the sky. I can hear his muscles snap with tension over the roaring wind.

All objects stop slightly, and then jolt into a hurried movement.

I curl my body up slightly when in the air, too much piercing wind, my skin will rip open. The trees flow below me, the mountains spring out in front. The Shingles rear up on the horizon, they look strong and high. The shore spins across my vision for a moment; it looks shadowy, sharp, and flowing. The airship tilts close, we'll collide soon. I look back down quickly to the trees, just one last glance. I see the graveyard and it's clearing, like an empty socket amidst the green.

How ironic, it looks so empty and meaningless from up here.

I twist myself and spin with all my strength. The wind blows back at me. It doesn't want me up here, not one bit.

I land with one foot, where the two black rails meet at a curved point of the bow. The deck's awkwardly empty. Only a flat, dark wood floor stares back at me confused. The rails are empty. No weapons fused to their rounded edges or decorative points. There are no doors, no portals, and no symptoms of entry into the howling craft.

It would appear this vessel serves as complete and utter decoy—no second or third doubt about it. Very impressive, very impressive.

I've seen decoys before. Does no one have the stomach to be original these days? They've built the ship with innards and hidden compartments, probably to protect them from the elements. The cold mauls and the wind cuts at this altitude, so it's a clever strategy.

I'm not able to withstand the cold at this speed and height.

I'm staring at the dark brown floorboards. They are slightly uneven, where each wooden block's shoved together. Clever—so very clever. I pull my sword from my back and smash the floor soundly. It was just hard enough to make the ship tremor slightly against the islands currents. A hissing sound steams from the boards, like condensed vapor being released from the contraptions bowels. I've heard the sound in war machines before. In one quick motion, an upheaval of sharp black pikes pierces through the deck in a steely synchronized movement. They sound so clean, so effortless. It's a clever trap, but it yields no results. Though the floor looks well maintained, the intense cold warped the wood, which gave the trap away. The spikes slowly retract disappointed and depressed.

I sense vibrations inside the ship; someone's coming up to see me. In the center of the deck a square door opens quickly. I move to my right quickly, running along the rail. A cluster of white, wide eyes peer at me through the darkness beneath the door. A thrumming sound suddenly drowns out the winds. A narrow stream of black arrows hits the empty air where I was just standing.

I leap into the air quickly. I spin as I'm in the air to create momentum for when I land. The wind whips my cloak and armor while I maneuver, but I stay steady. I am over the porthole. My leap has carried me halfway across the deck. A tall, broad shouldered man in brown platted armor storms out of the hatch running. I jab at him, and catch his throat with the point of my sword. His throat spills open in a contemplative deluge and he staggers back, gasping and writhing. He gurgles and trips head first into the hole. The heavy door slams shut as he tumbles down. I land on the square panel soundly, directing all my weight and energy to my feet. The ship stays steady and unhindered by my weight.

The floor shines so flat, smooth, and without error.

A splintered smashing sound echoes beneath my feet. I do not move. Yelling and screaming mixes in with the thrashing voice. Blood has squeaked out in narrow spurts, from the nearly invisible line bordering the square door. The soldier could only be flailing around down there. I punctured him just enough for it to be a slow, blood-filled death. I hear weapons scrapping wildly. This panic displays a lack of preparation that I wouldn't have expected in reference to my trap on the shore.

A man screams in a deep voice, must be the leader. All chaos ceases.

I move away from the door slowly and silently. I walk backwards to the rail and jump onto its black round edge. The wind curls my skin back into my blood. I jump off the edge of the rail and let my gauntlet, on my left arm, hook onto it. I'm dangling just out of sight on the airship edge.

The view of endless green tree's and white hills returns in a trailing flash.

Footsteps suddenly pound across the deck in irregular thumps. They're hard and metal; they nearly drown out the spinning engine below me. I'm impressed by their armor. The fusion of leather and metal isn't the easiest combination to forge. That little detail, along with this buzzing airship, makes these invaders very, very, enticing.

I'm debating my next move from my hiding spot.

I can swing up and kill the commander in one stroke, then go beneath the ship again to dodge the hail of arrows. Or, I can land in the center of the deck and allow their arrows to pierce one another in a mechanical crossfire. I could do this a few times, and it would reduce the numbers in my favor until they adapted to the strategy. However, either scenario seems rather predictable, non-elusive, and unoriginal.

Something clanks in the bitter wind beneath my feet and to my left. An anchor sits latched to the port side of the ship. It's black, wide, and smiling; it dangles just barely out of the wooden hull like an iron-forged raindrop. I grab the anchor with my left hand and tug on the chain. Something snaps and clangs inside, and the chain comes loose. The momentum of the chain falling immediately gets caught in the strong updraft of air, throwing it upwards and onto the deck into a wild windblown motion.

I can't see the result, but I listen closely amongst the howling.

Nothing, no screams, no broken bones, and no blood pouring off the side of the deck. The cat and mouse games were short-lived. With an enemy of this magnitude, phantom confrontations are sometimes counterproductive. I quickly crawl up onto the rail and peek onto the deck.

He has caught the anchor. It is the tall one from before, the one with the long feminine hair and black armor. The anchor looks toy-like in his enormous white arms. He's holding it like a child casually dangling over his arm. The posture's very amusing, and I laugh, but don't smile. He's so much taller than the rest, it's kind of astounding. Still, we're even ground, and I'll have the leverage on him. The brown armored grunts surround him with their crossbows pointing every which way but at me. They aren't looking close enough to notice my eyes peeping through.

I crawl onto the rail nonchalantly directly in front of them. The crowd of soldiers stare at me, none smile, all haggard grunts. They all look the same; silent, armored, white, and worn by the cold. I crouch down and point my sword at them. I level it, so it points directly at long faced commander. He smiles at me and shakes his head.

"Fire," he says solemnly in my language.

Before they're even close to me I have pulled my cloak about me. I feel the points glance off the impenetrable fur of Blue's father. The pressure from the arrows hammers intently, but the power of the cloak takes away any of the pain that might occur. The air hums with the adolescent rattles of strings and gears, followed by the thud of these arrows on my body. For all there imposing wails, the machines can barely push me back.

There are intervals in the chatters, reloading has begun. The barrage has turned to a slow and unsteady deluge. I fall off the rail unimpressed. I hear him yell, the captain, along with a garbled shout of commands.

I hook myself on the hull again.

I'm listening and feeling for where the gears and chains intensify inside the hull. I will damage the engine and alter the flight by changing how the ship's being supported. I hear voices above my head, they're looking for me. The air cuts my face and shakes me. I feel a hearty vibration with my left hand. That sounds vital, that'll do. I stab my sword through the hull, all the way up to the hilt. The machine groans slowly and I hear gears begin to click and howl.

That, by all rights, should do something.

Still, I can't be overly cautious in this situation. I must knock it off course completely. I crawl slowly back towards the spinning blades propelling this machine forward. I alternate hooking my gauntlet and stabbing my sword into the hull for support. The deafening sound of the fans rotating disorients me as I crawl. They're huge, at least twice the size of Blue. There are two stiff cords attached to the front of each spinning mechanism. I smile, they look useful. I sever them both with taunt elastic pings. The airship suddenly turns off course.

That was painfully simple and sublime.

I climb onto the rail quickly. There are two men standing, facing in towards the deck. I behead them with one swing, sending their heavy heads to splatter upon the deck. Their bloody bodies follow immediately behind, like they were trying to catch their freshly independent parts. I hear guttural, man-like roaring beneath me. Blue's following, he's close, and that's his signal. I wave my sword ever so slightly to acknowledge his advance. Men are screaming as they stare at the two bloody heads rolling across the rapidly growing red, deck. A man jumps off the edge of the airship in knee-limp fear.

I hear his scream end abruptly as he collides with the dense trees.

The commander pushes through all the grunts behind him and begins walking towards me.

A biting, tearing roar seizes the open deck. It drowns out the buzzing machine temporarily. A crashing form rips outward in the center of the men surrounding their leader. Screams erupt, along with the incessant hammering of their cross bows. To my delight the grunts have started firing arrows into their own brown-beetle ranks.

In short, Blue has arrived.

Inky, crimson blood pours and pools on the deck as the airship wavers and tilts. Blue uses his iron fur appropriately, shielding his eyes and head with his massive arms. He swings out at the men who have circled him trying to pin him down. His left claw connects with a tall soldiers white face, ripping it off in one flesh-wet, clean gesture. He grabs another man by the leg, with his other paw and begins swinging him around to give his attack more range in the melee.

I taught him that, I did indeed.

After a few swings the bloody deck clears around him, and Blue fetches another dead soldier to use. They go soft so quickly. No more grunts have come out from underneath. The few remaining ones on the deck have backed against the rails in a shaky line. They've pulled out their close combat weapons.

Clever, very clever, I've been aching to see this.

Most have plain and simple broadswords with clean silver blades. Others have short blue axes they might be able to throw if the situation called for it. None carry shields—an arrogance, a symptom of low expectations for me.

I won't waste my time one any of the grunts while Blue's here. One charges at me on the rail and I smash my hilt onto his helmet, shattering his skull and sending blood out of his eyes. Another one follows and I grab his wrist and send him overboard. Men are yelling incoherently as Blue storms around clubbing them soundly and methodically. The tall one does not yell, he's watching from the other side of the deck. I stare at him through the melee; he looks so feminine, and so delicate. It's an odd way to portray oneself in these conditions.

Blue continues to maul. He won't engage the tall commander. He knows I'm eager to fight him. In the past, most commanders have a trick or trap for the first soldier they engage. I don't want Blue to fall victim to them. The tall one has a spear; specifically, a long spear with a boiled, iron point and a round curling hook, like a severed eyelash. The point's clearly used for stabbing, and the curved piece of metal for slashing or catching blocking limbs. The spear spans twice the size of him. It's sickeningly offensive. If the opponent of the spear can parry the attacks and the weight, you'll become too confident and the moment you dodge the stabbing point, he can drag the hook into you from behind.

I've seen this before. It's nothing new or exciting.

More screams, howling wind, and waves of blood splashing against the deck. Blue has pinned a pile of them on the ground and pounds them with his curled fists. More men pop up from the floor, and fire arrows everywhere. I knock them aside with my sword. I break through the melee towards the tall one. He's waiting, but not moving. He looks odd, he barely moves his eyes, and they look like stained glass. A decoy maybe? I leap and take a quick, wide cut at him. I behead him in one swipe. His body promptly parts in half.

His skin splits in foiled, shriveled paper. The inside of his body bubbles outward in grey clay. That is a new one. I walk up slowly and part the body with the point of my sword. Wet, salty clay runs everywhere, and the paper skin looks flawless inside and out. A small vial in the center of his chest glows a strange emerald blue.

The air splits and snaps behind me in a heavy swing. Something's moving towards me, not an arrow, not this time. It's a heavy weapon. I spin and catch the object with my sword. It's weighted and sturdy. I can't let the weight pin me out here in the open. I let the object hurtle past me and through my cloak. It's the spear. Someone quickly swings the neck of the spear at me. I'm off balance. I catch the pole with my mitts. It throws me back violently. Blue darts behind me and catches me in his bloody paws, before my back even arches to the ground.

He looks concerned through his solemn blue face and bloody fur. I smile and wink at him.

The spear holder looks like my size, almost an exact replica in fact. His face falls narrow, scared, and jagged. His hair blooms upward wildly, in short and thin points. He has a bright red bandana wrapped around his pale forehead. It's for warmth I imagine. His plated armor gleams midnight black and grey. It covers his body similarly to the others. It looks worn, diced, and torn. Not much for decoration or utility.

I know this man's seasoned though, even without his mutilated armor. He has steel blue eyes. They're cold, cutting, and beady quick. I'm jealous. He smiles at me and squats down over the paper man. He sticks his hand inside the entrails and thrashes around. Then, in one quick jerk, he pulls the glowing vial free and throws it in the air towards the black rail. A pale white hand snatches the salve hungrily out of the empty air. The women, it has to be the women. She jumps up over the rail suddenly onto the deck. She stares at the wooden floor. It's bloody and speckled with bile. She looks pale, white, and piercing. Those strange blue-green eyes of hers, they almost glow.

She holds my eyes, I can't move them.

He stabs and swings at me. I jump back. The air hums beyond the black rail. More howling, and thumping machines drown out the deck. Men charge from our right, they feel invigorated by this man's presence. I push Blue howling into their crowd. The cold's searing on my tongue. More stabs and swings. He moves fast. I'm not intimidated, but impressed.

The air hums as the iron point follows me. It's a blur most the time, but I watch it patiently. I do not counter with my sword, but lean back and forth to each stab. I want him to hook me. He stabs impatiently at me and I swing my sword up quickly and counter. The metal clangs and echoes over the din. The hit staggers him, and he loses his footing on the slick deck. He wasn't expecting the power behind the strike. An arrow whistles at me, I knock it away quickly with my sword. So irritating, these interruptions of theirs. I charge the man in a big leap with my black shoulder forward. He leaps back, and lets his spear drift up nonchalantly. I quickly hook the massive point with my gauntlet on my left arm. He pulls me towards him by reflex. I smash the round, blunt bottom of my hilt into his armored chest. Not enough to kill him, but enough to wound. He jumps backwards a few times. He drops to one knee, and spits blood onto the deck.

He's smiling, why is he smiling?

She still watches, leaning casually against the rail. Something looks odd about her slender back hidden behind the whipping white cloak. I see a hint of metal below it all. The spear is at me. He has stood and recovered already. I'm very impressed. He swings at me, and I move. The rail smashes and sparks. The handle of the spear straddles to my left hoping to collide with me. My sword connects in a parrying vertical clash, only this time the spear bends and twists towards me. The spear's fast, it counters my quick swings. The rhythm and stances are quick for such an unwieldy spear, I'm impressed. He's smiling as we clash, so much smiling.

I'm proud of him in a way.

He looks very grizzly up close. The spear stabs at me again. I knock each thrust away casually with the point of my sword, while dodging the hook as he withdraws. The black point of the spear wrinkles blood worn, dented, and bent. He's seen many of me, but none exactly like me. The onslaught grows, but I show no signs of fatigue or irritation. The point stabs and I knock it away over and over.

He stops abruptly and jumps back towards the crowd on the opposite side of the deck. The wind screams, the motors hum, and the ship quivers in the current. He's panting like a dog; he's pulled his lips back along his teeth.

He's surprised by it all, and he's trying to conceal it.

The woman's still unmoved. I see her more clearly now since the sides have separated. Her left arm looks covered in a thin metal, like copper. It's a vile contraption, digging into the pale skin on her naked arm in greedy punctures. She suddenly bends over on the ground, the deck washing blood against her naked knees. She's hunched over the gleaming blue vial from earlier.

I love to think of what it can do.

The man still stares at me, trying to calculate and strategize I imagine. Blue has circled around towards them, pinning the entire crowd of peons against the rails. We've got them pinned, they're trapped. Blue breathes hard. Steam rises from his white hairy back. He's purring in a low song against all the bloodshed, it sounds peaceful, almost tranquil.

Ten men from the cluster charge him under a hail of arrows. Nine left, bones snapping. Six left, more blood rupturing. They're screaming, and their bones are breaking. Now there is only drinking.

What now? More are beneath the deck and back at the landing. It was a test, there are always tests.

The man with the spear stands up abruptly. He stiffens his back leg and crouches. I step back and keep my footing close. The rushing cold has turned the blood into a slick red walkway. He dives at me wildly with the spear. His attack looks undisciplined. This is my victory. I step back slowly as the spear grazes the air in front of me. I'm back against the rail, the wind whistles against its edge. I balance myself. He stabs again, in the same combination. I knock them aside easily—another ugly repetition.

I change my strategy. The hook, which is skimming the air behind me with each stab, is my move. I increase the parry and nearly assault him with blocks. He smiles and stabs faster at my chest hoping I'll eventually make a mistake. I twist my body letting the spear and hook pass me completely. I pull my sword in front of my chest, but just outside my shoulders. The hook hammers against it as he wrenches back on the spear. The sword falls out of my hands, to his angry surprise. I quickly catch the hook with my left hand, using the curled gauntlet as a latch. He slams the spear down on my left arm expecting it to be weak, but I can hold the spear above my shoulder rather easily. I crouch down violently pulling him off balance. I grab my sword from the blood soaked floor.

Still smiling though, he's still smiling.

He's aware of his the advantage with the spear. The distance won't allow me to slash anything vital as were hooked together. Still, stretching myself out, I'm able to slash his pale chin with the tip of my sword, and drag it up into his disheveled nose, nearly splitting it in half. Rushing blood hits his mouth and open eyes. He twists himself sharply and the spear breaks free. That's fine, he's disoriented, and I'll kill him in less than a moment.

An original yowl tears the air behind me. I've heard screams before, a whole orchestra of them over the years. I've caught long, loud, small, quaint, and gurgled screams—from every sort of man, woman, monster, and beast. I've never heard something like this before. It's her with the vial; the blue-green liquid digging into her arm. Her eyes have rolled back into white pearls. The whites are being eaten by glowing blue vein, which matches her little bottle. Her hair begins to split with pieces of blue energy falling between each blond strand. The veins on her arms glow furiously. They shutter wildly under the blushing blue. She bites her lip, blood trickles gently down her pale face.

She smiles—it would appear she can readily turn into a monster.

She kneels down slowly while staring at me and starts drooling blood. The weight of the airship tilts beneath her pale knees. The wind grazes the ship. The bodies roll toward the starboard side of the deck. They thump around noisily in wet smacks. They sound obscene against the howling din.

I can't directly engage her, it would be foolish. She's holding something behind her. It's not what I saw before; it's not that thin steeled-dribble of a sword. A ruse, a clever trick within a puzzle. An executioner's axe, I can see the massive blade poking out behind her little throbbing legs. It's got a long handle, brown and blood speckled. The weapon stands ridiculously big—a poor strategy for someone with such a little frame.

Still, it would be right if it was wrong.

Her body's veins are throbbing with little blue glimmers of dusty light. She pants hard in low, toothy cut breathes. More drool, but now it's freezing to her face. The weapon dangles lightly and casually at her side, like a shy behemoth. She stands and the airships weight shifts, more body's role. The strands of light in her hair hang and tangle against the breeze. The rails behind us creek against the cold, and the wind howls almost with her.

It likes her, the wind, like they're one and the same.

"Blue," I yell suddenly over the din.

He smiles at me. He's been sitting on the rail casually with his massive feet, watching the living fireworks. The blood has frosted in wild shapes against his matted fur. Gears roar absently as they try to find guidance.

"Engage her, engage her," I scream.

Blue throws down a man's back which he was feeding off. The dark jutted armor looks odd against his wild coat. He looks at her curiously, and tilts his bloody, smiling maw. His wild eyes judging her, even an animal can sense a woman. He throws the body at her in a grizzly metal flourish.

Good move, that's what I would do.

She cleaves it in two without looking up. There was no resistance to her stroke. The parts rattle against the deck in front of me. They were cut cleanly, without any error. She's something special indeed when paired with the hidden power in the vial. She leaps at Blue suddenly, clearing the bloody gap in one glowing leap. The ship shivers and she screams.

It's unnatural the scream, like someone being split in two slowly.

She swings eagerly in wide strokes. He leaps back, with his bulky arms covering his face from blood. The heavy axe moves back and forth, looking for Blue's throat. The sweep gets wider and more accurate with every pull. The axe handle's too long, Blue won't be able to judge it forever. He's on his heels ducking and bending. He leaps forward roaring, and bearing his claws wildly, and almost childlike.

I'm embarrassed.

He chases her across the deck, she is clearly baiting him. How infantile? This reflects poorly on me.

As they run I notice a strip of light against her delicate spine. I'm pleased by the spot. It must be where the artificial lightning runs. Filthy tools are incomplete. You can't hide the mechanical in the biological.

I will not let her cut down Blue.

His heels are growing raw. He teeters slightly in his swings. I pull my sword out from behind my shoulder. My wrist feels light. I'm nervous with excitement. I knew they'd have a trick, but its details were far more elaborate than I thought. I run full speed at her. I'm half corralled by my fur cloak, like the wind doesn't want me running. She whirls around to look. Blood has frozen to her chin in a messy trickle.

Even those small frozen drops are delicate on her form.

I'm to the midway point of the deck. She's there; she's bent down in front of me. Blue has stepped aside to the rail. He sulks lazily to the ground in a messy hump. He's happy for the intervention. She swings wide at me with that massive axe. I feel the sharp edge brush against my cloak. I can feel the harshness of the blade through the fur. It whistles through empty air—I can barely sort the sound out through the howl. I push her against the rail with my foot after her swing. I'm too close to cut at her. She jumps back cleaving down at me. The axe head falls directly in front of me. The metal's flawless silver, with small trails of stars and twirling designs. I pull the sword up crossways catching the axe right where it curves to the handle. I'm using my left arm. I need to test her strength. It was a foolish strategy. The axe pounds my left arm down in a thick smash. I brace my legs and my shoulder. The artificial strength, it's tremendous. I'm crushed downwards to the bloody floor. Blood from her mouth drips down and she bites at herself.

She senses the kill, she can practically taste it.

I'm pinned. My left arm shakes. The men are cheering her. She's screaming now, that howl stings my neck. She's an animal, thanks to that blue vial of hers. It's been a long time since I've been pinned. A random and unique tool her glowing strength. I nod to Blue slightly. She notices and looks at him excitedly. More blood drips. More glowing eyes shimmer. Blue charges at her, rattling the deck back and forth. She swings at him wildly. He immediately tilts backwards letting the cutting edge glide past his throat. She recoils immediately, her speed's uncanny. He's too close for her to gouge him with the giant axe head. She twirls smashing the handle into Blue. His forearms cross quickly taking the brunt of the force. The blow sends him rolling across the deck and into the rails. They break like wooden ribs beneath a mace. Blue thrashes into space puzzled and confused.

He'll be alright with his iron fur, it's like organic steel.

I walk towards her. I'll go half-speed. I can't show my true strength. Too early in the game for my full potential. I run at her dragging the sword point along the deck. She swings back at me too fast, she gets the timing wrong. I kick her in the stomach and send her backwards. She charges back swinging to my right. I counter the slash with my left hand, bracing my legs against the deck for leverage. It connects with that obscene axe head. My sword gets knocked clean out of my hand with a metallic slap. The blade spins surprised and lands in the floor.

How ridiculous, and how embarrassing.

She gawks at the stuck blade. I smash my shoulder into her and knock her backwards. The edge of my shoulder armor cuts her somewhere. I can smell the electric blood. She doesn't move. She's a living pillar. I hit her again with my left hand, letting the gauntlet connect with her stomach. Some skin is torn from her abdomen. I can see it on my arm. It's delicate, like untouched snow. She tries to head butt me. I duck and she rolls over my shoulder. She screams scratching and twisting.

An animal still, an animal empowered by some strange liquid.

I sprint towards where my sword's lodged in the deck. There are bodies clustered around it. I leap over them and pull the sword out in one clean movement. More screaming, she's behind me. I will not turn fast enough to counter any of her attacks. I whip my Untaro cloak at her from behind. I hear the axe head hit the deck. I turn quickly, kicking her in her hacked stomach. The deck shutters critically, the damage its sustained will cause it all to fall apart.

I'm running out of time.

I look around. We've already circled around towards the shore. I can see the seething black waves. She's on her feet and charging at me. I hold my sword with both hands. I'm leaping back between bodies. I want to connect, I want the contact. The axe, the power of the vial, I must truly test the strength. We connect, the wood shatters at our feet. The energy pours out of her skin, her veins, and eyes.

A sun lives within her.

My arms shake as she pushes, we're both beginning to wither—but she's decaying faster. I push her down to her knees in a quick motion. The axes handle rattles to the bloodstained deck. She immediately starts to look more normal, more human, the abnormal colors are fading. She falls to her knees sobbing wildly. Something stabs at me from behind. It's the unconscious one from earlier, the pushover. He's circling me, reevaluating his attack.

No time for a fresh engagement, pretty soon the airship will be over the sea and we'll crash amongst the white beasts.

He drives at me with the spear. I jump to the side and counter the stab. The tip of my sword cuts right above his eye. It bleeds immediately in a bloody flourish. The head always bleeds a lot. He steps back wiping his face. I stare at them. There's something about them that worries me, something hidden. The woman has started recuperating on the floor. She's still shaking over her knees.

Making monsters out of woman, what nation operates like this?

The man circles me again. I swear he looks older than before, and more grizzled. He might've of been bluffing about his ineptness earlier. He was scouting me, judging my strength. We'll have to hypothesize later though, the shore's closing fast. I'm on the rail. More wind, flakes, and cold. The green edges of the trees beneath us are dissipating quickly in flashes. The wind shifts east. I smile at them and fall off the side. It's cold and whirling. I watch the propellers as I fall backwards. They lazily fall off the black end of the airship. They groan and thrum ridiculously as they spin off.

The ship won't fall into sea after all.

I fall into the tree tops and spin my body as they release me gently into the snow. They'll survive the crash, I know it.

The woman, she was beautiful despite the blood, despite the blood.

Chapter Four

Haukter

I knew both would live. I knew it. The captain, the scarred and ugly captain, he underestimated me on the airship. He won't be doing that again. He bled for that mistake and he'll bleed again.

It must be humiliating for him to still be alive, especially in the eyes of his men.

The berserker, she was incredible. I've never encountered anyone before quite like her, especially one who can match my strength so elegantly.

I will kill her.

There are two things I won't do to the outlanders. I do not cannibalize and I do not rape. Either action breeds disgust, and would reduce my role to that of some raving animal protecting the city. I'm not an animal. Blue's barely an animal. I'm not an animal. I have witnessed and stalked a thousand women before. They've been dead or alive in front of me. They've been helpless and volatile, begging and fighting. I have never raped them. I'm not some maniac, some insect.

Cannibalism, especially when I began, seemed far more likely to occur. I eat every few days now, but when I first started running around the woods I was hungry all the time. I learned to fish off the shore. It was tricky to bait them into the shallows. I'd roast them during the day in the graveyard. At night, outlanders would follow the steaming firelight. I made that mistake a few times.

On the Shingles, the city people will leave me food in small wooden packs. Apples, cheese, milk and bread were the typical choices. Not much variety I'm afraid, but my palate might be considered unrefined, which makes it low maintenance.

When I was young I wouldn't conserve my strength. I didn't have any knowledge of appetite or eating properly. My sword would grow so heavy, so infinitely lead when I was starving, like one kill would equal one-hundred. The feeling ate me up inside. Only then, would the red meat slipping out of the armored cuts and severed limbs of the outlanders look appetizing. But I never succumbed, never desecrated the dead. I was tempted, very tempted. I could never eat the outlander's food. The security surrounding it was too much of a liability. Poison, toxins, traps—too many conspiring shadows to be considered with consuming their leftovers. Now, in the present, I eat only out of sustenance. And it's never come from another human.

The crash was a half-day's journey south of the wall. They must've steered the airship away from the shore before it fell out of the sky. They've built a little, round camp out of the brown and black wreckage at the base of a hill. Fires have been lit and are glowing beneath bleached white tents. Why are they always white? I don't understand the color. I'm tired of it. At the base of the hill, trees creep around them in uneven bunches. Their spiny clusters will be more than adequate to observe the outliers as they recover.

You can learn what type of patience an army has by how they recover from a defeat.

The men on the airship were just a handful of troops. Hundreds are pouring into the camp in long bulky lines. The white light of the sky and snow glitters against their metal trails.

Only two out of this collective mean anything to me.

Blue has been sour since his defeat on the deck of the airship. He's been sitting behind me in the trees. Small petals of snow have collected on his fur. Normally he shakes them off in irritating grunts and bumbles, but not today. He doesn't want to draw attention to himself, he's watching. He'll get his revenge—in time. Their survival from the crash doesn't surprise me. They certainly weren't pathetic or ridiculous.

Many have been. Many have been. I imagine they will be more tentative about another confrontation with me.

I wonder if they'll use this entire morning to recover. I slept a little last night, but not too much to cloud my mind. Blue slept the entire night and snored relentlessly. He was sprawled out on a pair of trees like a lump of furry rock. He's slept leisurely since he was young. Battling, killing, running, nothing has changed his ability to instantly sleep in any situation. I slept leaning against the concrete wall of the Shingles.

I can't remember if I was standing?

Sleeping has grown increasingly difficult with Haukter's prowls. Normally, I would sleep inside a hidden man-sized room in the Shingles, but the tightness of the space makes me restless. I've obviously outlived the desired size for that little cell. Plus, sleeping in a rocky tomb for thirty years can't be good for your health. I find random spots to sleep in no particular pattern, I must keep Haukter guessing.

I'm happy Haukter has no interest in hunting Blue.

Speaking of Haukter, I imagine he will appear to observe the outlanders. Such has become the tradition in the past. So interesting, so interesting he's decided to watch them. He never engages the encroachers in any fashion. This sinister stalking game he plays, I wonder if it'll ever lead to anything. Eventually, there will be no time for meaningless cat and mouse games. No time at all.

The invaders attempt to salvage nothing from the crash. The vessel was meant for combat, not transportation. The airship was meant to lure me out, to expose my presence to the invaders. A clever tactic, which I've seen before, they're not original. The men are arranging the pieces of bent, black metal into a wide circle. The soldiers in their plated brown armor look like fleshy ants running back and forth with black sugar. They'll be slaughtered like insects, squished and crumpled into red folds of metal.

The unsettling snow has been eerily constant since they invaders have arrived. The white sky has remained cloudy, boring, and irrelevant. If it weren't for the white sky and its dusty white petals, the green trees would never look luminous. We get light from the snow, but barely see the sun. It's been six days since we've had some permanent beams of golden light hang on the ground.

I hate knowing the days.

The Ills are probably moving inside the mountains right now, marching the grey tunnels and bleak cliffs till their feet are a pulpy raw. I wonder how many march. They'll want more vengeance towards me. I welcome it. They'll be rounding each corner with their jagged spears scraping the cramped walls. They'll cross every highland and high-path looking for me, peeking out from the shadows like tiny children in the night. I've watched them, watching for me a thousand times. It's hilarious.

The Ill's prince, the one who doesn't want any more blood, does he march with them? Does he know the corridors and tunnels? Does he know me? This prince might act more like a man than an Ill, but he's still a monster.

I need to change my viewpoint. I need to move to the left of the encampment, towards where the two commanders are resting. I'll let Blue stay here fuming in the trees. He's not needed for this part of the reconnaissance. I run. The trees rush past, no faces, just white and green gleams as I run between them. The troops are still pouring in from the shore behind them, hundreds and hundreds of them. One tent stands isolated away from the main body of canvased huts. That'll be them, I'm sure of it. I circle around and through the needling giants, and quickly crawl up one of their scaled trunks.

No one noticed me. I don't even need to worry.

The commander, the one with the spear, sits outside the folded entrance of the tent. The spear leans casually against his right shoulder and the black-hooked end slightly rubs against the white cloth. His withered face has been repaired from our earlier bout. Strips of white paper cover the right size of his face. He looks comical and plastic; I assume he feels that way. He didn't expect to be so easily bested during our combat. I could tell in his stances, he was caught of my speed and strength.

Now his face has been scarred with the marks of understatement and failure.

Did they really think an airship, handful of soldiers, and some bizarre berserker would be enough to bring me down? Has my little operation been such a farce? I have killed an uncountable amount of men. If I kept track, it would affect the outcome of my engagements with them. I don't need any other distractions.

I see her.

I can see her from the folded edges of the tent's entrance. A curled and silver lantern buzzes inside the shadows. It quivers against the wind, making me feel something in my stomach, some sort of memory. Maybe it's firelight, somewhere in the Diamond Town long ago.

Maybe it's nothing.

I can only see her hands or fingertips resting against her legs. Her body has been cautiously wrapped in thin blankets. There are long and narrow blood stains everywhere. I didn't inflict that much damage on her, the attacks were neither serious nor debilitating. It might be the vial? That'd be a wicked instrument. The metal delicately grafted over her spine must augment the transformation. It still causes injury though? The influx of artificial strength has drawbacks; specifically, your body being severely damaged and then being cocooned by bandages. How hideous? What sacrifice and idiocy for strength? The inhuman length some of these nations go to for these invasions befuddles me. Better to kill immediately then live with such consistent misery. I have seen similar tools used by outlanders, but never one quite this debilitating.

Her screams on the airships deck from before. They were cries, not screams.

I wonder how the inside of her tent would be like. Sterile, warm, endowed with herbs and candles to establish an atmospheric fog to accelerate the healing process. I wonder about the relationship between the two commanders. Too distant in the killing world to be romantic, yet, close enough to be a friendship. Obviously, they're a tandem in war. The man must have some intelligence, and his weapon—the spear speaks to complexity. Long spears are hard to use, especially in close combat with adequate precision. He's the trained killer. She's the berserker, the eternal trump card for all their engagements. She's meant to be wild, why else arm her with that enormous executioners axe?

To seize victory in combat, one must be honed in all skills, and not reliant on specialties. I'll prove and verify their shared ignorance.

There are screams south of the marching column where the forest becomes heavy before the shore. It's ascending, from noise to pure racket. The Ill's wouldn't venture this far from their black mountains to attack outlanders.

Haukter has come.

He waited till the column thinned and the last troops were making their way towards camp. There's chaos in the brown armored ranks. Men are yelling orders in my language. They have no idea what to make of him. The trees and forest crash around Haukter as he sprints. More screams and shouts.

He does look intimidating. I can give him that much credit.

He's a manmade beast, a skin-bearing spark of the harsh forest's fire. Haukter holds true to the dress-code of the invaders who abandoned him here long ago. He's covered in brown and black animal hides, which are composed of both skin and fur. How many layers encrust him—I don't know. On the uneven mountainous hides are layers of red feathers, and snowdrops of animals and fish skulls. They're bleached white to match the snow. The sleeves and legs of the sewn together hides hang past his fingertips and his feet. I would think he'd trip, but he's pretty graceful for a bulky bag. I don't know what's beneath the hides, but I know he has weapons, many hidden weapons. He wears a hood of dark black fur with three red feathers angle up in a quarter-circle. Just below his strange crown lies an opening for his blue eyes and narrow nose. Across his back sits a clump of antlers, which have been sharpened into boney points. The tangled bunch bristles behind his left shoulder menacingly. I wonder how he'll use them in combat.

It's all so very suspenseful.

He sprints at them directly. Not a single ant fires their pesky little crossbow at him as he runs. They're completely mystified by Haukter's appearance. He's too fast; they can't even form an armored wedge to prevent him from running into camp. A few men fire at him as he leaps over the wall of rubble from the airship. The rattling sound drowns out the screams of the men. The black arrows fly into the crowd of troops and skewer a pair of them through the chest. Thunderous shouting erupts from the other end of camp. Men part ways as the captain with the spear runs towards Haukter in an elegant plated dash. He didn't move that way when I fought him, he was holding something back.

Blue solemnly looks over the fray with his round blue face. His eyes glint against the white scene. I wonder what he's thinking.

More arrows fire and flap into the wind as Haukter charges. Haukter casually knocks them away with his massive sleeves. A majority of the arrows land behind his dash, he's too fast for them to anticipate their shots. A few clusters finally get the timing and unleash a coordinated storm of arrows. Haukter quickly stops and leaps into the arrow rain, shedding a brown layer of sewn animal hides in his wake. The soldier's eyes follow the decoy peppering it with arrows. There are hollow thuds echoed by empty air. It's a brilliant strategy by Haukter in a melee situation. He can shed those skins like the monsters do along the shore.

Haukter lands behind a line of troops and continues to run. A curved, brown wooden rod emerges from his right hand. A cluster of men charge him with their swords and some new square shields. They lock the brown scales of metal together into a trembling wall. Haukter swings the rod in a low arch at the men's plated knees. I can hear the humming sound of its slash through the chaos. Foot-long darts flutter out into the clattered column. The darts are narrow wooden points, with bursts of black feathers rolled against their ends. Men scream as the darts sink into their knees and thighs. The formations quickly shift their shields down as men fall down writhing on the ground. Poison, the darts are poisoned. How did he know about the blue flowers in the mountains?

Haukter swings the rod upwards in a blurred arc, letting loose another string of darks into the troop's gawking faces. Tongues, eyes, and mouths are skewered by the long darts. Men gurgle and fall, twisting around as their skin swells. They're all the dead and dying, the entire formation of troops. There had to be fifty of them at least. I'm impressed. Haukter runs past the writhing clump and towards the woman's tent towards the end of camp. He'll be there quickly. I start to draw my sword. I don't know why. The captain cuts the distance quickly. Haukter twirls the rod with a stinging hum. More darts cut the shrinking empty air. The man spins his spear leisurely, knocking aside the darts with the curved point. A few make it past the wheeling point, but the man just ducks casually down as the darts whirl overhead. One of the darts hits an idle soldier standing behind him. He immediately falls down, twisting and screaming in the patchy snow.

Haukter calmly reaches behind him with his left sleeve and digs between a pair of the hides on his back. He pulls out a colossal circular blade, which narrows to a sharp metal handle. The weapon looks like an axe head, only with no handle to balance out the swings and just a tiny tail of metal to grip it with.

The weapon looks ridiculous and unbalanced. I'm not sure what appeal he sees in it.

The man stops, pauses, and sizes up the weapon. A shadow trails the obscene blade. It looks like some sort of narrow chain or rope has been attached to the little drip of metal where Haukter grips it. The man motions with his pale hand to the troops around him. They quickly form another shield-locked line between him and Haukter. The pale man wants to test the weapon Haukter has just exposed.

The wind picks up, and the cold howls and shutters the trees. Good confrontation weather, very good.

Haukter swings the blade out of his thick sleeve towards the men. He doesn't swing the black chain a few times to gain momentum. He's got enough strength to swing the blade by himself. I'm impressed. The blade flies flat and perfect towards the line of troops. Haukter quickly pulls on the chain and the blade drops to feet level. The shields quickly adjust to the new striking point. The blade closes the distance quickly and just when it's about to collide with the clean brown shields—Haukter twists the chain and sends the blade spinning into the torsos of the men before they can even think. Limbs sever and split, torsos topple over, and blood spurts out from the line in narrow and wide gurgles. The ranks fall apart in split chunks. They look like sausages slightly torn open, with the filling falling out.

I hate sausages.

The pale and scarred captain has had enough and leaps towards Haukter through the hacked line. He leaps high in the air, arching his legs back till they almost touch the spear head curled behind his shoulders. He wants to test Haukter's leverage and strength. He needs to figure out how strong he might be beneath those animal hides. The brown hook and pointed spear curl down like a steel trap. Haukter leaps in the air abandoning gravity and leverage to deflect the coiled strike. A brown scaly sword peeks out from Haukter's left sleeve. The weapon looks segmented and divided into sharp-chunks, like squares of uneven bone had been fused together.

The two collide with a metal-laden thunder, so loud it shakes the trees. A wooden claw flies out from the other sleeve. It's massive, with each figure curled into piercing points. There are more than five fingers though; in fact, there are too many points to count as they blur about the air. The captain ducks below the flailing and artificial paw. He collapses onto the ground in a tight roll, his few pieces of armor picking up spots and streaks of snow. He's on his feet quickly. A man in the columns throws him a short-sword with a gold handle. He grabs the blade eagerly and throws it as Haukter lands on the red-blotched snow. Haukter twists nimbly aside with his wide form and the sword flies screaming into the white and green nothingness of the woods.

Haukter runs sideways into the columns, barely leaving any footprints in the trodden snow. I'd think with all those hides he'd be weighed down. The men dive out of his way in fear, not a single one stands to fight. He's luring the captain into the woods where he'll have an advantage in close range. Judging the distance between the trees, the captain won't be able to counter Haukter's attacks as easily.

It's a good strategy. Haukter's full of them today.

The captain follows him closely. His leg's strides are long and far apart. He glides over the snow like an ugly horse. He might be faster than Haukter actually, or at least when Haukter has been weighed down by the extra animal flesh. I must follow the chase. I can't let the show outrun me. I'm on the ground, and turning my boots through the jagged hills of patched silver-green.

The trees whisper about the fight, they want to watch too. They're always spectators.

Blue follows me. He's panting already in cloudy gasps. I don't know what's wrong with him. These chases and lifestyle, are they getting to him?

The troops bumble and rattle into the woods after their captain. A few fire arrows that pop and clatter into the thick trees. Haukter and the captain cross hills and streams quickly. The forest thickens to a maelstrom of velvety limbs and towers. Haukter stops abruptly and watches the horde of men approaching with their pale captain leading the charge. Haukter stands perfectly still, and in one large childish gesture, takes a deep heaving fur juddering breath. He slowly breathes out a small and dribbled cloud into the cold air. More arrows split the air in harsh black lines. A few come close to Haukter amongst the crowd trees. Haukter casually knocks them away with his flapping sleeves. They look indecent, like his hands were pads of dirty flesh. The arrows jangle dead and dainty against the sturdy trees. The sound echoes across the forest and tremulously through the endless snowflakes.

The captain has burst through the trees and into the cluster where Haukter waits. The captain swings down at Haukter again with the curved hook of his spear facing him. They clang again as Haukter's sleeve quickly swings up to counter the blow. Arrows fly in from the right of the combat. Haukter casually knocks them away with his good free sleeve and spins free of the captains spear. The captain quickly lays the spear across his shoulder and jumps into the air stabbing down at Haukter in quick steely bursts. Haukter immediately becomes pinned beneath the onslaught, and the captain lands leisurely next to him. Haukter struggles to match the speed with his enormous sleeves. The captain quickly swings the long spear around his body and off his shoulders, striking Haukter horizontally across the chest and sending him into the trees.

That's the strategy the captain should've have used on me. He used no strategy. I'm glad I saw this side to him. I knew he had it in him.

Haukter has leaped to his feet and charged the captain. Another good strategy, the long spear used by the captain has a disadvantage in this close combat. The wooden claw has dropped out of Haukter's left sleeve. It stabs and swings at the captain, who jumps back dodging between trees and branches. Men from the columns have routed Haukter, and charged in behind him to outflank his position. Twenty men rush with their shiny short swords drawn. They collapse on Haukter in one metal sparked clump. The grunts might have the upper hand. A few fire arrows crack into Haukter at nearly point-blank range. Their smacks echo across the valley and back to the shore and Shingles.

Everything echoes on this forsaken island.

Only seconds pass, and Haukter's curled beneath their stabbing mob. A low adolescent and unused scream splits the air. He doesn't have a man's throat yet? I'm glad to see not everything has been hidden away by those animal leathers. Haukter bursts into the air leaving behind a swarm of stabbing soldiers. Arrows follow the empty air and stop abruptly. The metallic thrumming of their crossbows echoes ignorantly into the valley. Screaming and yelling follow the swarm of men as they watch Haukter attach himself to a tree with his claw. Haukter has a hostage. It's a thin, narrow man, with green eyes and black hair. Haukter has the man by the throat with one of his sleeves. The man tries to scream, but the tension's too perfect. Not enough to kill the man, but enough to keep him silent and nonintrusive.

Haukter stares at the crowd of men and the captain, as his hostage shakes slightly against the high branches of the tree. Even if Haukter were to run tree to tree in elaborate leaps, the men could still follow him. Haukter must have another trick up his sleeve. The pale captain says nothing. He knows he can't barter with this random monster his army has just stumbled upon. He only watches, staring up at the hide-covered man, and guessing what new weapon Haukter might throw at him next. Snow falls listlessly. Nobody moves accept the man subtly writhing in Haukter's grasp. In one quick flourish Haukter swings his free sleeve and throws a cloud of black pellets into the air just above the men. They pop wildly and unceremoniously in the empty white space above the plated helmets. Bursts of red, blue, and green colors rain down on the men in powdery narrow streaks. The men scream wildly as the powder falls onto them, sneaking between the leather splits between their lashed and armored plates.

The powder has some sort of acidic compound to it. I can see their white skin boiling and roasting in the breeze. Their faces melt and curdle in elaborate bubbles. Only the captain has survived, having leaped away from the fray the moment Haukter swung his sleeve.

I admire his swiftness.

Where did Haukter get that powder? What far corner of the mountains did he unearth it from? Maybe he dug it out of the graveyard from his families lost expedition ages ago. Was he educated in how it worked?

Haukter has run away from the troops. He's running through the trees. I follow. I must follow. Blue follows me eagerly in leaps and hulking dashes between the trees. He's moving faster than usual. I wonder if he's apprehensive of Haukter.

I wonder if he's scared.

I try to move noiselessly, but at this speed it's nearly impossible with all the dry and frozen nests of broken branches beneath our feet. The trees are mixing into another again, only this time there are no faces, not a single one. Blue and I leap over hills and frost fallen trees. We glide between their columns and rows like quick, irregular images. We bound over creeks and streams. Blue staggers at one and splashes the water up in clapping burst. When that pure water catches the air, the lucidity of it stings, it reminds me of something. I don't know what, but some warm memory stirs beneath my eyes. Maybe it'll come to me.

We are halfway in the island with our stalking sprint— when Haukter abruptly stops in a thick bramble of trees. I crawl up a tree, a large grey one, which happens to be absent the spikey green. Blue wheezes and steams from the pace of our run. Haukter stands far away with his writhing prisoner. I can see him well enough from my vantage point. If this sprint might be some elaborate trap sprung by this masked monster, I want plenty of distance between us.

I watch. I must watch. What will he do with the man? I cannot predict what he will do; his whole presence here amongst the outlanders has been a bloody and poison pushed anomaly. Now he has one of them, and pulled him into the woods—I've been dreading this scenario.

Haukter's sitting between two massive trees. They're old enough to have lived through the first guardians, and the first Shingles. He's leaning on them casually with the squirming man, who slams his fists and armored arms into Haukter's thick hide. Haukter wraps the sleeve of his left arm around the man's face completely blinding him and choking him. He drags the twisting soldier over to a hewed black log oozing bits of moss. Haukter looks calm, almost methodic, like he's done this strange maneuver before. The man's becoming still beneath the shredded sleeve of Haukter's left hand.

What weapons does he grasp so tightly in the maze of cloaks he wears?

I've known the claw, the ridiculous sword, the poison darts, and patched hides he can shed so easily. What more tricks does he hide? I never knew he was this intelligent—I'm impressed by it.

The man, whose growing more still by every falling snowflake, must be one of their seasoned grunts. He's tall, wide chested, and long armed, but he still looks childlike against Haukter's hulking form.

Haukter rips the round-billed helmet off in one leathery crack. The man has a complexion similar to those who dwell behind the wall—white, dark-haired, and with weak eyes. Maybe they've come from a cold climate, which would explain their moderate resilience to the cold so far. For a bunch of ants they've made it pretty far into the island. Usually, I kill them all on the coast, but you can't always plan for perfection. The white monsters will be hungry in the blackness.

Too many outlanders for such endearments this time around—there are just too many.

Haukter stares at the man curiously from behind the narrow slit exposing his eyes. The man looks back at him with a mixture of fear and curiosity. I think he imagined himself being dead at this point. Haukter slowly moves his gigantic left sleeve above the man's quivering face. The curled brown tips of the claw slowly emerge from the sleeve like eager false teeth. In one quick motion, Haukter jams the wild edged claw into the man's mouth and bends his neck over his left knee. He gurgles maddeningly, as blood gushes from the torn edges of his mouth.

This grim operation makes me think of the time. The clouds are swarming over with small fingers of darkness. I watched their encampment in the morning, but it's almost evening. They'll be lightening the torches soon.

I look back to Haukter. He's raised his antler-armed hood slightly. The man still shutters between the two worlds, his eyes searching the tops of the tree's and shadowy sky. Haukter lurches over his throat. I can't see pass the hood. The man moves frenziedly, his arms and shoulders contorting over Haukter's strange embrace. The man would scream, but the claw muffles all sounds except for a desperate gurgle, which only a lasts a few seconds at best.

Haukter leers back quickly. A pink streak of tissue hangs from the bottom of his hood like a fleshy leaf. The man has stopped moving. A growing pool of blood brims around the round gash in his white throat.

Haukter's eating him.

Haukter's a cannibal. He slowly lurches over the hole—heavy with steaming blood, and bites down again from beneath his grizzled hood. He drinks, and drinks, and drinks.

In a slow lift of his massive shoulders, Haukter lifts the dead man up with his jaws.

Haukter's blue eyes quickly scan the snow filled canopy. He quickly finds our perch in this needleless tree. Blue begins to growl and bang the trunk of his tree with his feet. He can sense the confrontation coming. Good boy.

Haukter looks at me, and my memory drifts him back to the silly child I spared so long ago. He drops the body. The flakes and wind blow behind him, the elements themselves long for our confrontation. He stays steady in the vanishing light. He's a cannibal. I never would have expected it. He has no need for human blood. He could catch any food he wants. The skulls and feathers hanging from his clumpy fur are clue enough.

This game we play, the spying, it's all so very sinister. It will have a climax Haukter, it will. I fall to the ground, followed by Blue. I will retreat towards the wall. Yes, Haukter, you're hideous.

Yes, Haukter, be proud, you're very hideous.

Chapter Five

The Shingles

I haven't been this far back on the Shingles for years. Behind me the mountains split and open to the Diamond Town. The Shingles were built just outside the mountains narrowest opening. If invaders broke through the Shingles, they have to come through a narrow mountain path before they'd even see the Diamond Town. For years, they'd build wall after wall, line after line, to keep the outlanders from entering the mountains hidden valley. Now, all the protective chunks of mortar and limestone sit tilted and shattered, like broken down gates. From a distance and the sky, they must look like a senile predator's mouth with layer and layer of dilapidated teeth. Up close they're still imposing, but crumbling nonetheless. If they wanted to, the civilians could walk out of the valley and onto the path to the Shingles and see my black pointed shape standing here.

I don't know why I'm here.

I imagine there must be a reason, but currently it's not important. Knowing the reality of this island, all conclusions reveal themselves someday. I just wanted to stand where I could see the smoke rising from the city, and the orange lights bubbling in the morning gloom. I never take the time to look at it.

I don't know why.

I'm thinking about them, all of them. They're all out there. I can see their faces just by imagining them. The invaders are moving with their two elegant hounds battered and beaten, but leading the charge. The Ills, which now talk in my tongue, speak of peace and better things. I really haven't been thinking about them, and I really don't care. More wind beats the morning clouds. A slow trickle of snow glides down the needle trees.

Nothing changes, nothing changes.

Of all the views I can remember from my spying on this island. This view on the back of the Shingles where the first walls were built to keep the invaders out has always been the most lucid of the frontier. The white hills sparked with trunks of auburn and green. The ocean and its hard murky edge, like a dark disc at the tip of the always white horizon. For once, the forest teems with activity. It's not empty or absent. They're all out there seething, but I can't focus on them. Not one single bit.

Eight years, eight years, I have now calculated it. Eight years since I was last on this old wall, the first of the Shingles and closest to the Diamond Town. The food they leave for me has always been placed on the closest row of walls, a stone's throw from the frontier. This first wall hasn't changed at all either. It's grey, flat, and dull. A gap has started between the settling blocks. Along time ago, there used to be men and women who'd guard the wall with long pikes and arrows—until they started using me, and the ones before me.

The Shingles looks so empty.

The wind beats my face and throws my cloak violently. Blue stalks the woods watching the invaders and their movements. He'll come and report to me soon. I don't want to startle anyone from the town with his appearance. They only know Blue's species from being their victims in mountains and mines. I understand their apprehension. I would hate to be devoured by an untamed animal.

I will fall soon. I don't need much time here. For some reason, I keep peaking back at the town over my shoulder to where it blooms before the mountains. I wouldn't enter it unless I had no other choice. In my blood, very deep in my blood, it tells me to never go there unless needed. It's a hidden rule inside of me, a much hidden rule.

The wall aches such an empty feeling. I wonder how it looked when there were men along its crumbled edges. I cannot imagine how it would have appeared. The bricks have so many cracks on them, like tiny rivers spiraled through them. They leave behind darkened veins of decay. The grey's been worn by the wind in narrow rips. In time, it'll be powdered down like the white shore's sand. When a sturdy gust hits the line, the stones crack and groan. Someday it'll all sink. Someday it'll all be ruin.

I hear laughing at the north side of the wall where the Shingles mold into the dark mountains northern edge. Whispers, young voices, and small curls of giggling in the wind, it almost sounds like music. Some children have wandered up the steps of the first wall. A narrow trail of broken steps rises on the mountain side. The path connects to this particular row of jagged rocks. They found it, and climbed it. I'm impressed. I haven't seen human children since Haukter long ago. I've seen young Ills, but I try not to look at them very long. They have to die. They can't keep breeding and reproducing.

I can see their white foreheads and grey eyes peeking over the staircase edge at the other side of the flat wall. Their skin and eyes are nearly gleaming, and unspoiled. Would Haukter eat them too?

I would speak to them, but my tongue would be too heavy and unwieldy. I have not spoken to another human since my time guarding the forest. I want to speak to them, but I won't. They'll hear of me being on the wall. I stare at their eyes for just a moment, the jeweled grey lights twinkling wonder. It's a color I never really see alive in the frontier.

I fall.

The grey passes me in an endless sea of withered stone. The falling air drums against me hollow and dark, not the same cool lushness between the trees. Until I hit the cold ground nothing will occur. I won't have encountered or killed.

Haukter won't be out there waiting and watching for me. The vigilance can't be eternal. The fight will be coming soon. He's become a real, real, monster. The invaders will lick their wounds and begin moving. It's so ridiculous, so useless.

I twist my body to land on a soft patch of piled snow. It's in checkered mounds on the edge of the wall. I do not move right away. The shadow of this last Shingle, the original wall, it's cold.

I run. I'll move towards the mountains. Blue will watch the invaders maneuvers. We'll rendezvous at the river; from there we'll attack Haukter together and end this foolish game of predator vs. predator. I am slightly hesitant about engaging him. I'll need Blue's help. Haukter might be this islands personal definition of unpredictable. I haven't researched him appropriately, he's too stealthy.

I will kill him though, I will.

More running. The hills before the northern mountains are consistently random. Each white wave breaks and widens in awkward gaps. I keep running and even roll a few times to keep momentum. You don't want to lose your forward energy by hesitating. It'll be afternoon by the time I make it to mountains bowels. Last night was sleepless, especially after watching Haukter's evening meal. The always fickle sun might break through later; it'd be nice to see it.

I wonder how many Ills will have hoarded in the mountain paths. I'm sure they've grown quite arrogant recently. My attacks have been limited to the outlanders. They grow so insidious when they don't encounter me. I use to manipulate my appearances in order to draw large numbers of them out. When no outlanders are present, I tend to focus on the Ills incessantly. There are probably millions of them inside the mountain.

The paths in the northern part of the forest just above the graveyard, and where the river splits the island tend to be an Ill hotspot. They're always sniveling about in slimy packs. Sometimes, I have found the young ones playing between the boulders that mark the paths. They would kick a ball made out of leather and fur against the bits of grey stone. Eventually, they pulled their young back after a few unsavory incidents. I'm glad they realized how dangerous this island can be, it isn't the most suitable place for young.

The trails have some large boulders you can climb to get onto the mountains. Eventually, you'll hit a system of steps drifting even higher into the mountain. No Ills move openly on the steps, too many horror stories about me. In fact, there are still untouched lines of snow along the steps. Only the wind dares to move their clumps. Not a single footstep or sliver of untouched snow has been brushed by a brave Ill.

I reach the ridge where Blue and I slaughtered the Ills days ago. The blood still stains black on the stones. The sun splits through as I stare at the battlefield. The blackness turns to a dried red with foiled edges. The bodies are gone. They

111

came and dragged their dead away. It's slightly admirable. I'm not surprised, they've always done it. There are none around here, not a trap for me, no spears hanging off the mountains above.

I have to return to the forest. They'll be there, I know it.

They will be in the forest in a war party. It'd be slightly rare; usually, they tend to stick to the mountains. Haukter scares them out of the forest too. I imagine he tries to eat them also. The Ills move better in the mountains, since their bent bodies are better suited to running on cold stone. They look infantile between the trees. Animals walking and acting like men, it's hilarious.

I run.

I can already picture their scattering clumps as I approach. The Ills limbs sprinkling the fresh snow in spotty bits of red as I hack at them. Blue would be jealous I was hunting them without him. He'll shrug his massive shoulders, and rub his forehead slightly. He might even groan slightly in his throat when he finds the battlefield. His mannerisms are so human, so like me, it's hard to believe he's an animal. The drinking blood must be some deep-seeded tendency, which all the Untaro do when they kill their prey.

I'm happy for it.

I would have waited for Blue, but it's more important for him to watch and wait. When I was younger and wilder, I would cut the Ills down in melees without any strategy or plan. They started to lay traps for me with their largest fighters. Occasionally, in my youth, they'd manage a few stabs, scrapping the skin back around my spine and back. It'd be a nice little cut, and it'd give me enough bloodlust to hack them apart. There are scars. I use to look at them against the pool with my sword blade. If I turned just right I could see my nostalgic lesion. At the end of the slash a white tip of healed over skin glows.

It's never healed right.

I'm still moving, more rushing images through the trees, the same trunks, the same needle arms bumping up and down. The sun tries to break through the velvet canopy, but the yellow can't push the beams through the fogged-cloud ceiling. I wonder if the ground has had the sun on it since the island first broke free from the sea. It's not really important, I just wonder about it. Passing more hills, I'm heading south, back to the belly of the forest. I'll pass the pool soon and the edge of the graveyard. The shadow of the mountain draws back the more inland I get. The Ills will be here, they've got a sudden dose of moxie and it'll kill them. The hilt behind my armored shoulder keeps banging against me.

I usually run smoother than this, it's annoying.

They're here, I knew they would be. The Ill's, about forty of them clustered in a cramped clearing at the base of woody hill. I'll stay far away at first. I climb a tree using my sword as a ladder and spy the ground around the group. I breathe out a long breath; it glides against the spikey pyramid tops of the trees. The cold bites me here, it's getting worse, or I think it might be the worst.

The Ills aren't moving.

They're sitting down in bulky green lines. They're not hunched, bent or disfigured in their appearance. They look semi-normal for warty man-monsters. It doesn't matter, these columns, this possible evolution, they're still the same rats. They're still the same beasts. All are armored, but the plates around their bodies aren't jutted and crumpled by hasty forgers. None of the Ills in the front of the column have weapons, or any that I can see. I know I'm getting more paranoid about hidden weapons as the days go on. This could be a trap, there could be a thousand Ill's hiding further on in the woodland.

It has happened before—too many times to count.

I fall and break running through the trees towards them. I approach them openly; if it is a trap they will not expect an open confrontation. This tactic has worked in the past. I've used my ferocity to overpower the calmness required to spring a trap. A calm head during a slashing is a rare thing.

I move too fast for them to notice me from a distance. In moments I'm at their edge. One of the male Ills at the edge of the square screams at my approach. He's an uglier fellow with green bulging eyes and uneven fangs dripping onto his chin. He doesn't stand up or brandish a weapon. Nor do the Ills around him. I could cleave five at a time with the way they're sitting, but I don't move my sword. I stop and crouch outside of the living square. One of the Ills in the center of the square stands up and steps towards me. It's a male, he stands straight like a man, and the blemishes on his narrow face are non-existent. Another, more hideous Ill with narrow eyes, steps up next to him. He steps towards without fear, nudging aside his sitting comrades. It's borderline ridiculous. In the past they would stuff their corpses with a black powder, a compound susceptible to open flame, and leave them for me to find. Blue was obnoxiously good at sniffing out their traps. At times like these, I'm jealous of those animal senses. This Ill could be a sacrifice, a walking explosion, a suicidal paramour. This game becomes viler as time goes on, and this could be the oddest maneuver I've ever seen.

I must exercise caution. I jump forward and cleave the Ill in two.

Blood sprays wildly against the Ills sitting around the sputtering pieces. Two Ills at the very end of the line stand up quickly and run outside the square. They're very tall, as tall as Blue in fact. Even stranger than their enormous size, the Ills are twins. They're completely identical in every way, shape, and form. Each wears no armor, are covered in black tattoos, and their hair has been shaved in identical red stripes. They too have smooth faces, long noses, and big white eyes. Each one carries a pair of small battle axes, which might be used for both throwing and slashing. I have known about human twins before, even encountered them in battle. I've never witnessed Ill twins. I'm speechless, but I wouldn't talk to them anyway.

The columns suddenly rise and run away from me. I crouch back down with my sword point wavering between the snow flakes. More bits of afternoon sun pop through the thick cloud cover. In a few moments, the majority of the Ills are gone. The two brawlers and a much smaller one stay staring at me in the clearing.

I'm speechless. The one smaller Ill facing me, it looks just like a man, only colored the same villainous green. His face sits completely smooth, completely absent any blemish, scar, or bit of simmered skin. His body hangs lanky and slender, like a young man completely untouched by toil or strife. Royalty in their dark kingdom, that's what he must be. His armor shines platted polished silver, not the black and jagged materials I'm so accustomed to seeing. He looks like a man, an interesting image.

The two next to him are much more Ill. They're muscle bound, scar-ridden, and gleaming with a glint of war in their slashing eyes. They brace themselves in a relaxed fighting stance with their axes facing the woods surrounding us on each side. Not nervous these ones, they don't fear me or my reputation. These Ills are the royalties body guard, the elite troops of their entire hidden colony.

Hierarchy inhabits all living things, even these monsters I guess.

I'm vexed about how to proceed. It has been a while since I haven't been able to make an immediate decision. Fortunately, they do not sense my anomaly and only the sweeping flakes stir inside this clearing.

I unhook the black hilt on my black for my sword and grip it in my left hand. I might need the extra weapon for these two. I feel ashamed to use it so early on, but I've lived this long by not underestimating them. I flip the fur on my back around as I move to conceal the hilt. The bodyguard on my left taps the whelp's shoulder and points to the tree line behind me. I stand up slowly and use my tilted silver blade to look behind me. Nothing there, only trees, spilling snow, and flashes of green. I breathe out a long breath; it matches the clouds from the Ills. I'm jealous of their fantastic skin. It keeps them warm no matter what type of crawling cold. A form grows in the tree-line behind them; one of the bodyguards turns slightly to look. He's shaking—I can see his axes tremble. I didn't make them shake, and if it's not me or Blue, it must be only one person.

Haukter.

They badly want to run. I can see the trembling in their legs. They look back at me. Why is Haukter here? Why is Haukter always there?

It's quiet, no one moves, just the serene snow falling. Prey caught between two predators, prey caught between predators. Am I afraid? No, I'm not. I hate them. I hate them. I'll cut the Ills up till they're steaming slabs mixed in crimson slush. I will catch you Haukter, and I'll torture you, in fact I'll skin you. I'll throw the peeled skin into the water for the beasts to feast on, and I'll burn your furs. I hate him. Just one small act of charity in thirty years turns into the only who decides to hunt me. I charge the Ills. The one in the middle stays silent. Haukter, you should run. I'll kill them all. I'll kill them all.

The two bodyguards position themselves on either side of the meek one. I really want to cut him open. Haukter storms in from the trees like a hide-wrapped nightmare. His footsteps practically shake the ground. The bodyguards split, one faces me, and the other faces Haukter. My opponent immediately throws the axe in his right hand at me. It doesn't spin, but flies straight at me like a tilted blade. I knock the axe out of the air with my sword in a horizontal slash. The axe spins and smashes into my pointed-armored shoulder. He set it up to spin at me when I hit it. Impressive. The hawkish bodyguard lunges at me preparing to clatter. Something in my stomach stirs. I cannot identify it. I cannot understand it.

I jump over him.

He's as surprised as I am. I don't know why. I step on his face as I jump, which cracks his nose and bloodies his eyes. The crunching nose reminds me of old ice breaking on the river banks. His jaw doesn't break. I only wanted to stun him. I don't know why. I have never hit an Ill and have it live.

In the air, thanks to the springboard of the Ills face, I have brief moment to survey the situation. The other bodyguard has behaved in similar manner with the beastly Haukter, who runs at him like a storm of feather, skull, and hide. He throws his axe at Haukter who cleverly knocks it away with his baggy left sleeve, therefore preventing it from spinning at him. Why couldn't I see that? Haukter reaches behind his back and pulls another, yet different, ridiculously huge cleaver. It's the shape of a wide crescent, with a small dash of a handle behind its bottom curved edge. He must've forged it for days on end. Haukter throws the blade like curled lightning at the bodyguard. A thin chain follows the massive huge blade. He's able to manipulate the weapon in midair just like the other one, I'm impressed. The bodyguard freezes—I would too if I were in that predicament.

I don't know why, I really don't. This troubles me. Emotions are not always dependable. I'm between the blade and bodyguard. The shadow of the spinning blade falls onto us with its final turn. I hit it hard with my sword at an angle, so he'll have a harder time pulling the blade around to slash us. The counter with my sword isn't difficult, Haukter underestimated me. I know he'll jump in the air when the cleaver angles away from us. He'll need that space to maneuver it. I knock the bodyguard back with my left foot. I roll to the ground and hit the crescent blade again knocking it back towards the jumping Haukter. The crescent blade strikes his upper body in a vertical slash. Haukter sheds a flap of thick fur, letting the blade pass harmlessly by him. He's panicking beneath those layers and weapons, I know it.

I have a moment to hit him.

I've kept my hilt hidden behind my furry cloak. I throw it. He doesn't expect it, especially this early in the combat. I throw it perfectly straight. It's too heavy to spin. It hits him directly in the chest. Haukter curls up slightly in the air. He spits blood from the slit of his hood. It spills out over the leathery edge. He falls back to the ground stunned and on his knees. I'm running towards him. I catch my hilt as it drifts down. Haukter lunges at me, pointing his left sleeve at me. Exactly ten ribbons boil out at me in a writhing colored mass. They've got silver points on their ends. I knock them away from my throat and chest with a few full swings. They're extremely light. A weapon built for fluttering distraction, and nothing else. I look up from the tangled mess for his bulky form, but he's vanished. I see his shadow shifting between the trees ahead of us. Not as strong as I expected, and that wound might slow him in the future.

I take a deep breath and lean against my sword's handle. My knees are a little shaky, I don't know why.

The Ills behind me are silent. They haven't retrieved their weapons yet, but the bodyguards remain poised and ready to protect. The snow has stopped temporarily, and the sun has calmed against the thick eves. The Ill-man-child slowly walks towards me with a green hand outstretched. I throw a shallow slash across his throat. He falls to his knees. I don't know why I slashed him. The bodyguards howl and charge.

"Halt!" the whelp screams in a commanding, but gurgled voice.

They stop suddenly and help the cretin to his feet. There's barely any blood? Why didn't I kill him?

"He could've killed me, slit my throat, it'll heal," the boy says waving the bodyguards aside.

Silence crawls into the clearing. I don't want to talk to them. I never have. It's all very rigorous.

"In the mountain—," The boy gurgles through the blood and cold.

"I don't really care about what you have to say," I say deeply against the snow. The sound of my voice surprises them and me.

"Ten years I have waited," he starts again.

"It means stop talking," I bark.

"What then? Another lifetime of silence?" he snivels back.

This was a bad idea. I'm out of my element.

"In the mountains, that one who attacked, that's where he's been," he says elegantly.

"Haukter."

"What?"

"His name is Haukter."

"How?"

"I named him, I named him," I shake my head with this answer.

"He's not with you then? How do you know him?"

"I know everything, now stop talking."

The bodyguards bristle at my arrogance. I could still bleed them both.

"Why do you think I'm here?" he asks in a thin, dying bird voice.

"To die, bleed, be cut, or killed," I laugh at him. My humor surprises me.

"You don't listen to anything, what should I expect out of you?" he asks.

I laugh a little harder. I lean on the handle a little more vigorously.

"I don't have to listen, and don't have to do anything you don't do, and I'll kill you." I laugh.

The boy looks around at his bodyguards who shrug their shoulders apathetically.

"What?" he says raising his thin eyebrows.

The snow starts again. You can smell the water on the air.

"You don't need to talk, talk is you being useless, you need to act. If you act more, you'll be more. If I hadn't acted, you'd be dead."

The prince turns to his bodyguards looking confused and questioning.

"But what now, we're speaking, and it's not bad?" he says.

"It's seems redundant though. I don't really care about what you have to say."

The goblin boy's well-educated, he's kept me engaged.

"Then why even talk," he barks.

"You wanted to. I already knew we were completely unable to relate, hence why I wanted to kill you."

"You're a fool." He spits.

I stop leaning on my sword. I stand straight up. I can feel the forest glittering behind me. I really want to kill him. I still don't know what stops me. He narrows his eyes at me. I wonder what he's thinking.

"We're more like you than you can imagine, and I'm tired of it all. My ancestors were too. I'm tired of it all. No more killing." He says solemnly.

"Now who is the fool?"

"Someday you will be gone, who or what will carry your standard?"

"I don't care about then, only now."

My stomach feels unsettled. It's trying to calm me down. I don't know why.

"I can do this forever. I know every snowflake, every shadow in the woods, and all the frost in the mountains."

"Nobody knows every snowflake. Every single snowflake's different."

I want to kill him. It would be silent. It would be nice in the clearing.

"Things are changing. Even you can't stop it. You seem intelligent enough to realize this," he speaks proudly.

I really want to kill him. I can barely listen to him.

"To be honest, I can't really focus on anything you're saying." I mumble to him.

"Oh no?" He says. He smiles a white line of perfect fangs. Not all human yet.

I start to circle them slightly. I need to take control of the situation. The white snow crackles under my feet. The clearing seems much larger than before.

"You may not understand this, but whenever I see you Ill's—I just want to kill. It's a complete compulsion, and it's very hard to ignore."

The bodyguards start to widen. They still don't trust me. If I wanted to kill, it'd be done.

"You are a monster," the boy says.

I laugh.

"Not only that, but so is Haukter, only he's a real monster, and I made him. He will probably kill me."

The Ill prince looks surprise.

`"Kill you?"

What's the point? This synopsis, this summary, and this entire conversation.

"Yes, kill me."

New concern drifts over his face. The blood from his small wound has run down onto his armor, and the fur behind it. Perfect depth on that cut for him. It'll heal fast, but it'll scar. It'll remind him I spared him.

"I really don't care about anything you have to say."

The Ill sighs and shakes his head. This whole conversation for him has been exhausting. There are strange roars westward in the forest towards the shore. The outlanders are moving. Why hasn't Blue retrieved me yet for us to attack? Did they slip past him? Did they kill him secretly? I've stopped walking. I can feel the snowflakes bubble onto my head and melt. A few drift past my hair and onto my skin between my tunic and armor. It'll be evening soon. The darkness will make it harder to move and to fight.

I put my hilt back on my armor and swing my sword through it in a flourish pass my shoulder. I laugh and walk towards the prince. I look at him closely between his simmering guards.

"You're a prince right?" I ask.

He looks surprised.

"No, I'm king," he says solemnly.

The machines throw some metal thunder down from the cloudy horizon. Their rumbles echo off the trees. I shake my head to myself and smile.

"I guessed wrong," I whisper.

"What?" he says.

More booming howls from the western forest, I know the outlanders are moving before nightfall.

"I am a very curious person about machines and such." I say to the King as I walk away towards the forest.

Still more awed silence.

"We give them our flaws—make them walk and kill when we cannot. Our skin isn't hard enough, so we plate and armor theirs. We cannot fly, but we give them wings."

I run into the forest.

Chapter Six

The River

Where is he?

Blue, where is he? The river, I told him to meet me at the river. It's the only river on the entire island, the only frozen spine. He understands river, I know he understands it. I'm at the eastern edge of the river. Behind me the woods sit sulking. Past the woods are the Shingles, mountains, and the Diamond Town. The river runs from the northern forest, southward, and then into the Diamond Town. It's mostly frozen, but still not safe to walk on. I could walk on it, but Blue would make the crusted white crackle, and the plates would split apart. Normally, the island never freezes like this, and the black water runs constant. Too cold, it's been too cold; I've known the river like this only a few times.

Still no Blue—only snowflakes and the evening trees.

Why is he late? It's been an eternity since he's been so late. I can't stand it. I want to beat him for this. That seems excessive considering the circumstances. I just hope he's alright, or the outlanders haven't captured him. He's too quick for their feet. There are booms and crashes on the westward side of the river. I'm up high in a cluster of trees on the opposite side. I can hear the pressure changing inside the forest. Something screams mechanically, it's a strange howl which screeches over the river echoes.

I fall to the ground with a slight thump.

Light suddenly splits at me from the other side of the river. It looks like a glowing blue eye from the still velvet woods. The needles part from between the barky stems. A stretch of ice suddenly splits a narrow slit over the wide river. The treetops explode above me in a blue blast of frozen wood and needles. Snow hisses and falls downward in uneven lines. It's falling towards me, the spiked and shattered limbs. Something grabs me and hauls me to the side. It's fast and soft.

It's Blue.

They've found us, or to be more accurate—they've ambushed us. Not the typical behavior of outlanders. Steam rises up in pillowed geysers on the westward side of the river. Roaring has begun, gears stubbornly mashing against each other in the cold and frost. I can see their brown armor reflecting in the fading sunlight.

The woods split in front of me, bending like water against their contraptions.

These machines are dull looking things. From afar they look like blocky, rounded fortresses. The body becomes wide and awkward where the legs come to the ground. The armor has a dusty brown color to it, just like the troops, and is excessively plated so black lines give the appearance of scales. The legs are bent backwards, like if my knees were reversed. Atop the legs sits a mechanical clump, where the pilot operates the machine. It looks like a curled fist on top of two flimsy bird legs. The pilots head and torso jut out unprotected from the base of these mechanical walkers. In the center of the protruding chest are three long pieces of metal which are curled back. Behind the petals of peeled metal an emerald light shimmers. The barrel chest must literally be barrel of a gun. That's probably what shot that blue-green fire at me a few moments ago.

I'm so happy the pilots sit unprotected above these walkers.

In all fairness, they probably were built with the idea that infantry would never get close enough to attack or mount the machines. From my watching spot, I can't see the backs of the machines, but I imagine the false guts are there, since steam drifts up in narrows wispy gulps from their backs. The image of the machines marching across the shore isn't disorienting. The waves of snow falling from the trees aren't either. It's the sound—a random groaning mixed with an aching metal sound. The roar groans and questions like the metal itself knows it shouldn't be moving under this weight.

There are twenty of the machines. They're spread apart in the tree line. The commanders will not put them onto the ice. Blue and I's best strategy would be to lure the grunts out and drown them. On the ice I can kill the two commanders, the two anomalies. I'll instigate the machines, and use their booming power against them.

I must generate some fire.

There's a group of fresher needle trees to my left. Their stalks only stand about twice my size. I quickly begin slashing at their bases with my sword. They topple cleanly over. Blue reads my mind, and grabs the trees as they fall. He catches them in his giant paws and then holds them in the middle for balance. He's a smart animal. Bursts of frost-rattled explosions surround us in bright flashes. I've noticed a whining sound preceding all of blasts. A hissing sound, which rattles like stretched water. We can't stay here any longer. I think Blue has all to ammunition he'll require.

I'll draw their fire.

I run along the forest edge at full speed. I don't want to fight them in the night, even with the torches. The popping blue light follows my every shadow. Trees fall, needles cinder, and snow bursts. They cannot hit me, they aren't even close. Blue has followed the path of bursts. He's hiding in their smoke and billowed debris. I turn back as I run, he's got a tree ready, and it's sitting across his shoulders between his muscles. He throws it leisurely into the air in a wide arc. The machines try to adjust their angle of fire, but miss the spinning log. The blue orbs twirl into the sky and vanish into green lines. The log curls towards the massing troops. The shadow looks graceful on the snow and trees, it looks so innocent. One machine fires a last shot and blows apart the log in the middle, right above the huddled troops. Splinters fly everywhere, knocking men down and blinding them. One chunk of the tree crushes a man into a bloody flap atop one of the machines. The other chunks rolls over some men and knocks a machine over, which crushes the man in half.

Their screams echo nicely across the river.

Blue doesn't stop, and the machines haven't refocused their range of fire. Another log flies through the air and onto their formations. Another machine gets crushed along with a group of men stationed around it. The machine fires as it get pulverized, blowing aside skin and bone in the troops lines. I laugh. A few of the brown-plated men are injured. Their compatriots run over and fire arrows into their skulls with their crossbows. No room for mercy in this battle.

That's something to keep in mind.

The machines reform their line and lower their chests to the ground. They're stones, living stones awkward and clumsy. They hiss again, and something wrinkles the empty air between our two riverbanks. Arrows, thousands of them, shot and sprayed into a continual stream. The black arrows block out the white light shimmering upwards from the icy river. There are too many to knock away with my sword, or fur cloak. Whatever contraption spins in their chest, it really thrusts their arrows. The trees split and sever under their cloud, like pillars of easy ice.

I split back running into the deeper part of the forest, too far for the arrows to splinter the trees and stab me. I wave my sword behind the green-layered underbrush. Blue runs to meet me in a furry flourish. His man-wild body looks quick, bulky, and fearsome. I'm proud to have him here with, so very proud. He runs in front of me and I jump onto his back leisurely. He puts his paws beneath my feet and runs back towards the green explosions, and streams of arrows. We get to the shore and the white water valley, and in one quick paw flourish, I'm in the air flying over the river.

The maneuver was too quick for the invaders to see our nonchalant piggy-back ride. The air above the river and tree's feels quick and cold. Below me are hundreds of rows of troops. Brown line, after brown line, after brown line of troops silhouetted. The snow whips my face and bashes my shoulders. Humorously enough, Blue quickly rolls into a ball and topples over the river bank and onto the ice. He keeps momentum, so not to shatter the ice beneath his bounces. His body has a muscular coarseness to it, along with that iron webbed fur, causing arrows to sprinkle off his bowling form as he moves. The insect's fire at him constantly, but that doesn't slow his spinning.

None look up above where I'm sailing across the empty space—except the man with the spear.

I'll have to land in the middle of them; at a long distance Blue and I are a liability because of their ranged attacks. Up close, we'll have the advantage. I whistle a piercing screech at the grunts below with my two fingers. I want them to look up and fire, so their arrows fall back into them like pointed rain. Several of them look up and fire at me with their mechanical crossbows. Their clatters follow me up to my high air. I knock a few away with my sword. The rest fall back towards the troops in screams and punctured skin. They lose track of me in the sky, thanks to this deadly rain. The man with the spear screams at them under the inconsistent hail. A few arrows fall his way and he quickly spins his spear knocking them away.

He knows they fell for a very easy trap.

I play the wind for just a second as I fall. I need to fall in line with Blue, who has almost reached their columns along the westward bank. I position myself just a quick jog away from Blue inside the swarm of troops. He won't be too far away thrashing and mangling on the edge of their encampment. A walking machine sits directly below me with a pilot who can't seem to adjust his bulky range of fire. I check the location of the man with the spear before I land. I need some moments before I engage him in our final bout. He's too far away to engage me right now—lucky me, lucky me.

I fall on this machines poor pilot in one quick weighted stroke. I slash downward as I collapse onto the walker. I cut the man in half between his eyes. His halves curl and splash into the troops standing around the machines squared edges. They panic immediately; they've become less seasoned throughout their visit to the island.

Haukter might've had more of an effect than me.

I'm in the center of the infantry host. The machines are spread out far apart enough to not pose an immediate threat. The grunts don't get their arrow guns around in time to point at me atop the machine. I slash downward in a whirling arc, cutting a few faces and throats. I slide into the cockpit of the machine and quickly whirl the half eggshell around to point into the rest of the troops. I don't really understand the whole sea of dials and levers at my fingertips, so I start to hit buttons randomly. The machine suddenly crouches down and fires a long stream of fluid arrows into the horizontal columns. Men scream and fall down either silent or gurgling. I can see the blood trickling points plucking through their skin in bloody spots.

I smile.

Two machines have worked their way towards me in the melee. One stalks in my shadow, the other sits directly in front of me. They start to glow blue-green fire. It collects around their peeled cores in translucent streams and smudges. I quickly tilt the machine over and leap off. The two orbs streak through the air and destroy each machine in a verdant flourish of crackling power and metal. Idiots. They've lost their edge completely. Their commander must be ashamed of how they're behaving.

I'm running through the clouds of brown armor now. I've got my left shoulder down to cut or stab any man which steps in my way. My sword slashes up and down as I run, cutting men left and right. I'm too close for arrows. They'll hit each other in the crossfire. They're also too slow to pull out their swords and swing around their shields.

I had such high hopes for them.

I behead a man in front of me. I leap of his stumped body and grab the crossbow out of his hands. I fire one solitary shot in front of me. The heavy weapon clatters awkwardly. A man falls down impaled in front of me. I grab his crossbow before it hits the ground. I have two now. I fire in all directions around me, unleashing a wide circle of pointed stalks. They fallback like a brown wave on the heat of my spiked shore. The crossbows metal chamber hammers back and forth. The screaming brown shapes topple against one another. A massive clump has formed directly in front of me. Blue's just beyond me, attacking and carving away at their outer lines.

I hope he's okay.

They've started to out flank me in this melee. One crossbow crackles empty. I run into the crowd so they can't focus fire on me. I bet they're willing to sacrifice a few men to take me down at this point. Where's the man with the spear? What's taking him so long? I run. I leap off the pile and separate myself from the gathering collisions of armor. I can't expose myself to their bum rushes any longer. The other crossbow twines empty. I throw it towards the men behind me. I make my way towards the river. I'm not far out from its icy billows. Speaking of which, where's the icy woman-monster hiding? She has yet to make an appearance. I leap over the last confused soldier before the river and jump down onto the ice below. It's empty quiet, and absent any blood—for now.

The peons haven't even turned around to me. The bloodshed spooked them even further. During my flight towards the river, the machines realigned at the front of the army to powder the river with their pretty lights. They roar and grind as they center on me on standing on the river. It's too late for them. Screams hit the air.

Blue has fallen upon them.

I run to join him. Blue's strong enough to throw and swing the machines freely in his enormous paws. They howl and groan under him as he grabs and tosses them into the scrambling men. Men scream too, firing arrows randomly into the air. I'm running towards the muddled edge of falling machines. He grips the machines at their backwards feet. His paws look small against their metal extensions, an enemy worthy of his size. He strains under their weight; you can actually see the lines of his muscles and veins beneath his fur. He balances them, smart boy, one in each paw. He can only spin them twice before he scatters them in each direction. The men fall like blades of ice cracking and shattering in bloody streaks between their shells. Four other machines are smashed and turned over. The men run from the colliding metal monstrosities. They run onto the river in a wild panic. The shore and tree's ooze red in extravagant patterns.

It's quite the sight.

The ground troops are collecting again further down the shore. The man with the spear has taken control of them. Swarms of them hiss and dive at his blood painted form. He barrels forward to take away their momentum. They scream and yell. The arrows mix into each other making a confused black cloud.

Two of the machines have turned to me on the river's edge, just south of where Blue attacks the troops. They fire a paired stream of orbs at me like stretched thunder. They move too straight, too stubborn. I run in-between them as they scorch towards me. My sword is out in my right hand like a waiting needle. I need it to balance me out as I move horizontally between these blasts. The ice below my feet bursts and cracks against the round fire. The white ice pops and splits. It will all come apart. The cold water sprays under the deafening air. The sound annoys me. I weave my way between the bursts. I can see the surprise on their goggled white faces atop their machines. The wind whips the spraying water, it nearly freezes in midair. The machines groan and bend down, unleashing a fade of arrows against me. So annoyingly predictable. I'm in the air before the metal rods reach me. I'm a little late in this jump. The arrows are against me in a pointy wall. I'm caught in the tip of the storm. The momentum pushes me back. I whip the fur cloak out in a wide arc in front of me. Arrows break and clatter into one another. A few stranglers spear at me below my cloak and I knock them away with my sword. They shake my sword and sting the handle.

They underestimated my ability to jump at the onset of this battle.

The black storm takes a large amount of my momentum in the air, pushing me back against the shattered ice. I spin my cloak again and knock more arrows away. Troops have started to run onto the river. They're tired of watching the slaughter. A middle-aged man with a short sword and broad shield rushes me. He's a fool—brave, but a fool nonetheless. I impale him with the long hilt of my sword and kick his body off onto the ice. They surround me, and crowd me, on both sides of my shoulders. I cleave in a wide sweep leaving my feet and spinning forward to face them. Only limbs, ligaments, and blood remain in a motionless pile.

Where is the man with the spear?

Blue has collapsed on the troops north of me like fire on ice. They look like tin little toys before him. His nails, thick as iron and sharp as diamond, form a talon whirlwind blurring around his muscled form. They fire arrows at him in the maelstrom, but he keeps his left shoulder hugged to his face. A few arrows have pierced his hide and blood smears on him. The arrows don't slow his relent, and his nails rip strips of skin with lines of red tissue and white string. Normally, he's not this wild, but he may be blood wild. I should allow him more activity at healthier intervals. He's driven most the men around him into the woods to recuperate and strategize. We've done well with our kill ratio, but there are still many more left alive.

A sole arrow whistles at me from behind. I can feel the splitting pressure of it. I turn barely in time and knock it away with my blade. The collision slams heavily and the arrow falls steaming into the river snow.

The man with the spear has fired it—a nice shot.

He's standing on the river quiet and stern. The shore next to him brims with his troops and machines. The surface of the river has cracked and sways under his weight. They're making some formation on the shore, some pointless maneuver.

He stares at me, the pale scarred snake. I'll kill him.

"Halt," he yells. His voice sounds thicker than I thought. Still no sign of her.

"He's my opponent, I will not share him," he barks turning to his peasants on the shore.

I watch him carefully, waiting for a trap or plan. I'm cold, but my back sweats steam. I never use to sweat like this before. Blue's still attacking their flank on the shore. They've surrounded him in a wide circle. They're too scared to jump in the blood-ring with him. Men are screaming, their arrows are rattling.

"Halt!" He yells again.

The ants slow their slashes and arrows. Blue tears one of their faces off with his right paw. The soldier screams then gurgles. Another one comes to his aid and gets torn in half. How embarrassing.

"Blue!" I yell. He has grabbed another man with his left paw, which completely covers the soldiers face. He pulls the grunts head off quickly and bounds onto the river in bubbly bounces. He leaves red paw prints as he runs. The headless body he just produced pools an eloquent red smear. Blue's covered in blood. I wonder if he's surprised to hear me yell his name. I don't think I have said it in years.

"I prefer for an unspoiled conflict," he says. His voice has a husky highness at the end of it, like he's asking a question.

I don't say anything. I will not say anything. I walk out onto the shifting white plates; they stir and sway on the black trickling water. The grunts bristle and murmur in the background.

I'll kill all of them. This is ridiculous.

"We learned your language you see, we captured one of your ships ages and ages ago, you see?" His voice mixes sharply on the wind. Blue makes a throaty growl behind me.

"You can understand me, can't you?" He asks.

I begin to walk closer to him. I leap to the closest round shield of ice. He crouches down slightly judging my distance with the pointed hook of his spear.

"I'm glad we could meet like this, they talked about you in legend, and you're a worthy opponent." He says sternly.

More circling, and more walking around the flattened ice looking at one another. Blue has withdrawn from the shore. He's behind me now balancing his size on the river. Good boy. After I kill this man, the ants will try and storm us from the shore. We won't have a chance on the river with this host of troops. We'll withdraw into the forest to wait and stalk. We're invincible in the underbrush.

Except for Haukter.

"Where I am from, where I was bred, it's impolite to not greet your opponent," he says condescendingly.

I stop walking on the snow encrusted ice. That's the best reaction I can give him. It pleases him well enough, he smiles back. Actually, it's less of a smile and more of dried smirk. I'm not overly confident in this situation. I'm always calculating. He wants some distance for the first collision. He's got the advantage with the length of his weapon. I check the shore for her blond hair and pale skin. Nothing there, just the man and his drones, that'll have to do.

He's directly ahead of me. We're standing where the river bends out wide, and the two shores are at their most distant separation point. I didn't plan the maneuver at the onset, but I'm happy to see the vast amount of space between me and the western shore, which has been lined with his grunts. The wavering of the ice and its lack of balance works in favor of the spear. If he's able to pin me on the ice he could drown me or throttle me. A good strategy.

"Once again, I'm glad we met. I had only imagined some fabulous monster out here in these woods. I'm pleased to see it's only one man with a pet," he snivels.

I choose this moment to charge him at full speed without a single glimmer of hesitation. It feels good to move this fast. Everything blurs, the water hums below my feet as I leap across each misshapen piece of ice. I'm in front of him in two jumps. He has barely finished speaking when I hit him with my sword in one quick little slash. He's surprised and leaps backwards with the point of my sword nearly tickling his throat. He quickly sprints sideways in his cluttering armor and runs across the ice. He's trying to distance himself from me. I take a quick horizontal slash at him again as he widens out. The point clips just below where his armor curls onto his shoulder. It'll sting and sour when he lifts or balances his spear.

I break away running after my slash. He charges after me and we dash across a few of the sheets. He jabs at me quickly. I block the closest stab with my sword. The strike comes from his waist. He doesn't have the best leverage. The strike rattles my sword and palm slightly. It feels good to have pain. The stabs are full force, not like when I nearly killed him earlier. The spear breaks after our weapons collide. He attacks again and I counter with both my hands on the sword. The spear wavers loose and weak in the air from the counter. He can barely keep a grip on it.

We break away again and immediately start running.

He smiles more as we run side by side. That idiot smirk, his contempt makes me proud in some way. I'm buying time with my sprint. I'm waiting to judge his style of attacks. I'm sure I could kill him. It's the grunts and crazy woman I'm concerned about. She might make her little cameo when this duel concludes. She's quite the unpredictable variable. I will kill her. I just don't have an idea of when.

He leaps at me across the turbulent sheets. They're quivering with each movement. He uses the tail of the spear to spray snow at me, to obscure my vision. The head of the spear stabs through the splash of ice and snow. The steel around the point and curved hook looks old, worn, and chipped. I knock each stab away with quick vertical slashes. I have to concentrate; it'd be easy for me to fall behind. I backpedal across the chunks of ice. He chases with his stabbing spear piercing only empty air. He's very fast and competent this time around. I'm excited to truly fight.

I break quickly to the left when he recoils one of his stabs. It gives me enough space to counter the spear. I swing

143

right and he moves the spear vertically. The slamming collision jars us both, and whining metal fills the air. I continue swinging at him, but he back steps across the plates. I chase. I'm swinging wildly almost. I'm getting frustrated. Be calm I tell myself, calm. He's contorting his shoulders sideways to avoid the blade. He's smart. The long edge of it misses him each time, whistling empty air irritably. He can't use the spear to counter, it's too awkward. I'm too fast and he knows it. He'll eventually run out of maneuvers. The chunks of ice beneath are leaping feet bend awkwardly in our maneuvers. He stumbles slightly in his metal boots. I take the opportunity to slam my knee into his chest. This knocks him off his feet and onto his back. I stab down towards him with the needle point of my sword, which looks accurate and true.

I hit open space again.

I shouldn't be surprised. I didn't expect to kill him so early on in our bout. He's too experienced. I'm not surprised.

He's rolled out of the way and jumped away on the scrap of ice next to me. I currently have pure momentum; he's recoiled too much and has to play defensive. I jump in the air to swing down at him. He leaps at me, recoiling his back and arms in a backwards pale curve. He's trying to gather enough strength to hit me with a pounding vertical hit. He moves quickly in the air, but I move faster. I swing crossways using the opposite force. They connect, and the iron clangs maddeningly as the spear flies three plates away from our spot in the air.

He jabs his arm at me. A thin, brown piece of cloth has been wrapped around his pale arm. I didn't notice it before. He pulls the cloth away from his arm to reveal a collection of sharpened points and chains. They fire at me in a metal pointed clump. They don't separate very well in the air. I swing the Untaro fur against them as I reel back. It blocks them easily. The spring-loaded force from the weapons causes the points to get hooked in the fur. He wrenches on the fur with all his strength and sends me flying, trying to create a greater distance between us when we land. He needs time to grab his spear. I'm through the air spinning calmly. I'll fall down quickly.

He lands on one of the floating sheets about four leaps away from me. The spear sits beyond him by the same amount. He runs towards it immediately. I follow, running sideways across the ice. I'm doing this to intimidate, to match his speed in a more relaxing posture. To his credit, he continues to be focused on retrieving his spear. He runs wild and inarticulate, like flailing strips of pale armor.

He's starting to panic.

I don't want to engage necessarily as we run. He's unarmed and that mode of combat tends to be unpredictable. The wind blows wildly. It whips my skin and boils my hair. I am sweating beneath my black armor. It's tedious. I break towards him. I swing straight and thin, it could cut anyone in half. He ducks quickly beneath my blade and tries to jab me with his fists. I follow each move with my hilt and knock them aside. The punches are quick, but not desperate. He swings his body around in a wide kick. I brace the black metal of his graves against my arm as the leg connects against me. The weight bursts against my arm, which trembles slightly in response. He's strong. I knew this already, but it still impressed me. I throw him off of me, and he rolls across the ice. He's up and leaping to another sheet before I can even blink.

The repetition of this chase isn't enticing whatsoever.

He nearly has retrieved his spear. I follow him and match his speed. I slash at his belly in a killing swing. I slash and the snow howls. The black, plated armor splits open behind my swing. Harsh white skin beams out exposed. No blood, guts, or bile.

I'm awestruck. He managed to swing his stomach back moments before I landed the strike. No more underestimating him. He's reached the spear. He has the spear in his right hand and he back jumps away from me. He stops and crouches down on the ice. I follow but misjudge my leaps. I'm too close when I land on the ice beside him. He slams the spear down on top of me. The weight of the swing gives him speed. I brace myself as the strike hammers my sword into my shoulder. The round hook on the opposite side of the spear forms the bash. He twists the handle of the spear to hook my sword. I pull him close with my right arm. I can't move, and neither can he.

We are deadlocked.

More snow falling. I have to think. I have to contemplate. The plate we're standing on bobs on the black water threads. Nothing else moves. We're both quivering as we lock our weapons. Blue roars wildly by the westward shore. I respect his anger and encouragement.

"I know all about you," he grunts. His breath coils out in a cloud.

I stare at him. I want to speak to him, but it would be inadvisable.

"I should say we know all about, all about you and this."

I continue to stare. It's a wild conversation without me even speaking. No one, save that Ill prince recently, has ever mentioned to me what I do here. Not in plain speech.

"I know what you are and what you've been doing the Branch has been watching you for a hundred years. They have studied you and your predecessors. You've been dissected. We've even learned your language."

I don't want to speak, but he's using this conversation against me as a distraction. I must answer to consume his concentration, not mine.

"And?" I say softly.

He smiles slowly as we struggle.

"Aren't you even impressed I know you're language?" He asks.

More silence, I have no reply.

"We know who you are, since they were patient with this island. They've been testing it for a hundred years. They've even hired a few invasions to come here and learn the layout."

I've had enough. I push him wildly with all my force. He nearly collapses, but keeps standing.

"The layout of course," he laughs back.

I've become angry. It's not uncommon to have people talk to me, convinced they know the island back and out. This isn't the first conversation like this. Truly, it isn't the first.

"We know all about you or the people before you. The role you play here, it's been this way for years."

Lies and truths.

"You're a number in the line of many. We waited for the coldest winter and came. We figured it would slow you down."

The fool shares his strategy. It will not affect the outcome. He's panicking deep down.

"Okay," I say.

He's no longer smiling.

"It should be an honor, if you know what that means, that I've come here to fight you."

He licks his lips at me through a white smile. It's disgusting.

I break the deadlock in a flutter of iron and snow. Enough playing games and investigation, he needs to die right now. I shove him over. He spins at me stabbing the spear. We break from our stances and sprint slashing at one another. The diving spear follows my dashes and scrambles. The pain of each clash rattles across the wide river. He chases me back across the plates towards where the troops and Blue are watching us. I knock his blade away some more. We get to a few uneven plates. I start slashing at him wildly and vertically. This has been hardest melee since we've started fighting. He's panicking.

I leap in close to him and spin my sword around narrowly. He's too close to pull his spear point around to counter it. He blocks my quick slashes with the handle of his spear. I kick him in the chest, blood sprays out comically from his mouth. I'm not pulling any punches now. He falls down and scrambles away. I stab at him leisurely as he crawls away. He knocks my blade away with his hand and kicks me in the stomach. I cough, the pain feels good. He's up and he's holding a knife in his hand. It's curved and long. He slashes at me wildly.

I was arrogant.

I retreat and run slightly. I need some distance for my sword to be able to block that knife. He leaps at me as I withdraw. He lands on top of me, grinding the knife into my blocking sword. He has leverage; my strength can't keep up with him. My sword presses against my chest already. He's going to try and throttle me with my own blade. He'll kill me and take the city. Calm down. Calm down. I pull my left arm free of my hilt and double my strength to my right sword hard. It's the last of my strength in this lock—I don't have anymore. My gauntlet on my left wrist sits curved and perfect. The hooks are round and sharp, ready to catch any blade or scrap of flesh. I slam my left arm into his face. The pain doesn't stutter him. He doubles his strength and my sword gets rammed into me, bleeding into my armor and my first layer of skin. I'm such a fool.

Keep pushing me down feel safe captain, feel safe.

I hook his right cheek with my gauntlet and wrench his face around. I knock his knife away with my right foot as I twist him away. I stab him through the chest quickly as he falls over, a slow wound, enough to by my time with the grunts response on the shore.

A scream blasts on the west river bank. Snow whirls around the river like its terrified. I'm on my feet now. The river shutters some more, like it were running from something. Another explosion on my left, black water flies everywhere. I feel the pressure of the air bubble towards me.

It's her.

The howling stretches animal-like and wild. The axe guides her, its hammering ice as she runs. Her strength brews water clouds. I follow her spring from the riverbank towards me. Someone else screams. It's him, the pale dying one, he's still alive. He charges me swinging that knife. It's wild and undisciplined slashes, like he wants to die. He knows it. I knock the knife away with my sword. The curved eyelash of metal falls into the snow casually. He coughing up blood and panting like an animal. I pull him close to me as he staggers. My gloved hand wraps around his throat. I stand up straight and hold him high. We have nearly the same build, the same features, it's eerie. His eyes are glossy and fading into a faraway blue. I pull him close to the Untaro fur shielding my left shoulder and back. I know it feels warm to him, I know it. He's gasping at me. I shake my head. He smiles slightly. I open my mouth to speak to him, but her screaming interrupts. She's coming.

I stab him through the heart. I should've cut off his head to demoralize the grunts, but I couldn't do it for some hidden reason.

The men on the shore yell and scream. The ice veers up as she lands behind me. I turn. The air swirls in front of me. The axe twirls too. I throw the man on the outside of the plate into the trickling black water. He deserves some type of burial, and this is more than I usual give for the dead. I retreat from the bloody stain below my feet, leaping backwards onto more ice sheets. She's covered in bandages, but still looks monstrous, fiery, and wild. I still can't believe she wields the massive axe. It's very ridiculous. She's gaining on me as I retreat. I'm moving towards the largest plates of ice. She won't be able to shake or bend them. The axe blade whistles towards me, I can't run anymore. I swing my blade crossways connecting with her wild slashes. I give it all my strength, and I match the direction of her slash, this will take some of the momentum away. Sparks boil and the force shatters the ice beneath our feet. She's beautiful. I break the clash and push her away with my foot.

I don't kick or punch her. I don't know why.

I hear something in the woods. Someone's moving inside the trees on the eastern shore. It's not Blue or the Ills. I break from her as she reestablishes herself, and I sprint to the eastern side of the river where I was standing before. Something's moving shadowy and quick. I see a large form swinging, a muddled hand flails. It's Haukter. Something red and wild bursts towards me from the forest line. I feel the pressure and the air changing. I need to move. She's on top of me again though, and my sword swings up to meet her latest strike.

We lock again.

It's in my neck, in the skin beneath my hair, between my armor. It's a brown dart with red feathers. I bite my tongue under the pain and blood simmers in my mouth. Blue roars. I twist with all my strength and send her toppling in a bandaged, blue glowing mess. She lands on her feet not far away. I pick the dart out of my neck in a bloody pop. Blood trickles down onto my back. Poison, I must control my blood; stop it from assimilating this vileness. The world flows uneven and rushing, all the whiteness and evening light mixing together over the black-broken river. I hear arrows firing towards us. The sound doesn't match the world around me. I look back towards the shore. He's gone.

How did he hit me? She's running at me again. I have nowhere to go. I par her swing. I can barely stop it. I kick her in the stomach quickly. That's the last of it, the last of my strength. I fall to one knee on the drifting ice. The snow falls delicately, it looks more detailed to me for some reason. I hear men yelling. She's screaming. Something roars beside me. I'm off the ground. I cannot stay awake.

How did Haukter hit me?

Chapter Seven

Blue

There is something cold in my mouth, it tastes gritty and bland. It's dirt. I move my mouth slowly and carefully. It's all I can move right now. My throat stings and bites me. Something heavy pushes on the inside of my skull. I've never felt like this, it's a unique sensation. I move my mouth some more. Something long and fibrous fills my mouth.

It's Blue's hair.

After a few moments I begin to stir under my lumpy setting. My body has been curled up; my knees are against my chest, and my arms are wrapped around them. I struggle slightly to move anything; my strength has been sapped because of the poison. It'll come back, it didn't kill me. I'll cut you to pieces for this Haukter. I will. No more pity from me, no more pity. I breathe some more in the darkness, more strength rushes back to me. I can hear the wind bustling off the shore and the wrestling off the waves on the rock. The shore billows half an island away from the river where we battled—how did I get here?

I start to wriggle my arms free of the weight. My hands are around my ears. I touch something smooth and round behind my head. I panic.

"Blue, get off me, I need to move," I gurgle.

No reply, only the crashing of the waves.

"Blue, please get off of me, I can't move. I can barely breathe."

Still, only silence and wind.

I feel around the back of my head, and I know it's his face. I try scrapping his round cheeks in the darkness.

No response.

I'm angry. A strength flows into my chest, some sort of will, it presses against my ribs and stomachs. It's coming back, all that fitness in the cold, the hidden fire. I want to throw him off of me, but he might be hurt. I can't hurt him anymore. I start to uncurl slowly and carefully. Something long and floppy falls to the ground on my left letting cold air inside. The frigid air startles me like acid. My skin's still sensitive from Haukter's poison.

I'll kill him for this—I have never wanted to kill something so ardently.

The weight on my back feels less and less. I'm regaining strength by the second, a vein flame burning bright. I stand up slowly, letting the mass carefully slide off my back. The white daylight burns my eyes and my head throbs for a simple, confused moment. A group of velvet trees are tower over me, watching me, spying me. I am in a clearing near the shore, just a few high hills away from the black water. I can see the black waves shifting in the white spaces between the trees. I fall to one knee. I stood up too fast, blackness bubbles in from the edges. The snow beneath my feet has been dyed in discs of red. My stomach sinks somewhere into my spine, and my throat tights up into my jaw.

Behind me, Blue is dead.

His body has sprawled out now that I have moved. His back sprawls a frosty, raw red. Every scrap of flesh, every scrap of skin and sinew had been hacked off. There are arrows, probably close to a hundred, peppering the fused chunks of red. They must've shot him after she'd cleaved as his back with the ridiculous axe. Those arrows could never have pierced his hide alone. The damage to him shimmers disgustingly vivid, was this necessary? I will kill them all for this; specifically, I'll cut them to bits and feed them to the monsters along the shore.

He was the one, the only one who cared about me.

I pick up Blue's massive paws. His iron nails are all gone, all torn out from slashing and clawing. The wind turns quiet while I look at his hands. They look gentle and soft without the nails, like they weren't the hands of some beast.

I watch the snow falling carefully. The pace and snowflakes nearly match the flurries from before. Not that much time has passed. We confronted them in the late afternoon and early evening. This must be the next morning, the very edge of dawn. It took me that long to recover from Haukter's poison? The invaders will be attacking the city now; they'll have needed to recuperate from our battle. The

Shingles probably stopped them in the dark. They'll have waited for new daylight.

Blue's round face looks so small against the red snow, so frail and little. He's smiling beneath the fur and blood.

Why are you smiling Blue?

I have never buried anything before. In fact, I have seldom known dirt before. Only when a few of the encroachers have used weapons, which bite the earth in fiery explosions, have I seen bursts of it. I've never buried the encroachers either; the corpses twisted and preserved by the island cold are too powerful and persuasive.

I drag his body closer to the cliff, to where the trees break completely and you can see the waves and shore. The sun continues to fall lightly between the clouds over the shore. The daylight's wandering randomly, like its gleam won't take hold on the island. I cut through the snow and ice frozen into the ground. It takes a few slashes till I can see the livid brown earth beneath it. The soil stirs dark and mangled with wormy roots. I use the point of my sword to cut through the veins and pull the dirt towards me. The hole barely widens, the ground's hard and stubborn.

How did he hit me? Nobody has ever hit me from far off. I just handled him earlier without any problem.

I'm sweating, but it's still cold and frost biting. Why am I sweating? It's dripping down into the hole. It's still not wide enough, my sword's too narrow. Why did they have to kill my animal? More sweat, more scraping of the ground, I must widen it now. My swords heavy, I drop it and tear off my black hide gloves. They never should have hurt him, he wasn't truly a threat. My protégé, I formed him, I commanded him. Why did they mutilate him so? They knew he would die, why would they mutilate him so?

More rage through me, I'm losing control as I dig. The hole has become massive, deep, and dark. I sit down quickly. I must relax. I must relax. Life has misery. Misery has life. Blue will no longer be here. He's no longer here and his pain's over. I must finish the hole. They will hit the Shingles and walls next.

I relax. I breathe heavy. My hands are shaking.

My hands start digging again, only they're calmer and slower. I need to contemplate my next four moves. Haukter must be killed, he's the chief threat. He hit me from far away. No one has ever done it before. The confrontation in front of the Ills earlier where I crushed his chest with my hilt and bled him, it must've been a ruse to lower my defenses and expectations. He was building my confidence.

Awfully smart, awfully smart.

The hole grows even bigger. You could fit me inside now. It's a nice place for you Blue, away from the mountains, memories, stalking Ills, and cold graveyard. We're too far from the rock empty part of shore for the invaders to notice your grave. You won't have to notice them either; it'll always be a luminous empty shore for you to watch. It's a good spot Blue, a good spot.

His body feels lighter than his frame would imply. I'm still weak from Haukter's poison. I drag him to the frosty edge and tilt him over into the hole. He falls and the trees shutter slightly, some old snow breaks from their high tips. The snow falls on him inside his grave, it looks peaceful, a natural serenade. His body curls up slightly inside the hole. It's a little too small for him.

He still looks frail inside his grave, so very frail.

Filling the dirt's much easier, much easier. It only takes a short amount of time till the dark dust has covered him completely. The top of his grave looks exactly like overturned dirt and nothing else. I don't like it. It's not clean, but filthy and unkempt. It doesn't honor him at all. If there were rocks nearby me, I would outline the spot. Of course, who would come to look for him? I already know where his grave will be. Only his father knew of him, and I killed his father.

His father, I will leave him a piece of his father for him.

The snow still drifts the same cloudy pattern. The daylight falls down quietly like vented silk. I lay the silver Untaro fur over the overturned dirt. Much better, much better. I use some small pieces of sharpened wood to pin the fur into the ground. They're tight enough for the cloak to stay still in the wildest of winds. The grave looks pleasant. The snow picks up as I stare at it. It's growing colder too. My breath hangs like smoke in front of my eyes. My back feels light without the fur. I'll miss the protection I had with the fur. My black armor looks oblong without the cloak. The black spike on my left shoulder looks uneven in comparison to the rest of my plated armor.

No matter though, it wouldn't be right to use the fur.

I stare at the grave, nothing moves, nothing happens. I have to leave, though, I don't want to. I have to leave Blue, but I don't want to. At least I can leave you with a piece of your father Blue. At least I can do that for you.

I run.

Haukter will be around, when I do not know, where I do not know. I don't really care either. I will kill him. I will kill him. The tree's bow before me dark and black, I'm cutting through them as I run. I imagine their roots and rings have lovely details to them. I've never examined them closely. I don't know why. It's getting colder. This might be the coldest it's ever been.

The natural world has its own sense of irony. I'm learning to enjoy it.

It'll take me a little while to reach the Diamond Town, even in full sprint. The time seems like a minor epoch, but I will maintain my run, I will. Blue ran me halfway across the island with a shredded back. Quite a distance, and quite a remarkable thing. I'll kill them Blue, rest assured I will kill

Haukter. The paths between the trees are becoming cloudy as the sun blooms the new frost. The sun rarely shines like this so early in the day. There are always storms at sea to block out the sun.

How did he hit me?

I knew he was strong. I know he ate men and Ills. I even suspect he intimidated Blue and in an open confrontation with him would've been killed. Yes, most likely. The encroachers will be a match for Haukter though if I should fail. The man with the spear was powerful, he may have made Haukter nervous, but he still would've been defeated. The man with a spear was a specimen. I have not had competition like this since I first started fighting in the forest.

Haukter, a minor transgression, has been groomed into a major inconvenience.

How he became this strong I don't know. He's a complete and utter mystery to me. There are no mysteries on this island for me. I've had to know everything. It keeps the Ills and invaders at bay. It could be in Haukter's culture to survive? The ability to learn in new and foreign environment, those tendencies would be good to know. Too bad I killed his entire clan and kin. Sometimes, my long term strategies are rather faulty. Who would have known there'd be something in his blood which would make him so tedious and tenacious?

You sleeping fools in the city, you have no idea what awaits you. The Ills could also kill them; quite easily in fact, the townsfolk would be no match for them. I left the conversation with the Ill prince rather abruptly. I did not kill him or his bodyguards. I hope he understands what my mercy meant.

I look behind me at the shore. It's just a dark line on the tree washed horizon. In a few moments it will be gone. I am getting close to the graveyard. Then I'll hit the river, more woods and valley, and finally the Shingles. I can run a little lighter without the cloak. I might be hit by their arrows, but I'll just have to be extra attentive. I haven't run like this for years. My chest feels heavy and the air coming out of my nose steams back into my eyes. The cold air bites my chin, and shreds my chest. I cannot feel the ground beneath my feet. It's there; I know I'm rolling past the cold, veiny terrain of this island. In the Diamond Town, the land looks much different.

Only in the Diamond Town.

The trees and their needle-blankets whip against me annoyed and grumpy. I scatter them with my sword. I never let go of it when I passed out. Shadows are filling up the spots in-between. Almost to the graveyard, almost. The light really hangs on the trees. I've never seen it like this in all my mornings. Ill omens or good omens? I will be to the graveyard shortly. I will rest momentarily there. No point to me appearing exhausted at the time of battle upon the wall. I was already across the island when I woke up—in the complete opposite direction of the Diamond Town. My lungs feel weak and limp from the poison.

No matter, I will kill them.

I can see the shapes of the graveyard ahead of me. They're rather angelic, yet ghastly in this luminous water glow. The encroachers probably shivered at their appearance. I'm halfway there, the graveyard happens to be the grizzly midpoint to the Diamond Town. I designed it, or it was designed this way, by whoever came before me. Unfortunately, I don't truly know my role in all of this, or how many came before me.

I remember, back in the city when I was young—very young, some sort of ceremony was happening. Everyone was there, every single citizen of the Diamond Town, and there were flags everywhere. They were the color red, the only time I've seen that color other than mixed with blood and muscle. There were lines of little boys everywhere, including me. There was some man wandering along the line. He was gaunt, hunched, and twisted over like the withered corpses in the graveyard.

Speaking of which, I'm here.

Not sure why I am staring at it. The graveyard looks solemn in the sunlight. The objects look lonely and ominous. The snow falls peacefully on them, like it's waiting to jumpstart a tempest. The graveyard waits for me. The machines, the skeletons, the men, women, animals, they're all there. Some were before my time. My blade never touched them. There are even more buried beneath the snow.

How they got there, I don't understand.

The shapes, they look more mutilated than usual—more distraught. It might be the light. They would be ghosts in the night. They look so real, like they could shake off the ice and come to life.

It's tedious, very tedious, to see them like this.

I'm breathing hard, even though I have stopped. That day so long ago, I remember the lines of boys on the wall. It was snowing, lightly, like this. I remember it perfectly. They were walking so slow along the lines, the old men dressed in red. They were carrying pots, or metal cans. I don't really care what they were, it's an annoying detail. They had coals in them, blue coals with specks of red magic. Some instrument was playing, a stringed harmony mixing with the snow. They were dropping the coals on our outstretched hands. All the other boys would scream and cry beneath their orange glows. It was quite the pathetic display.

I have stopped breathing hard now.

They outliers will reach the city shortly. I'm still far behind them. I'll kill them at the Shingles, or inside the city. I have never done this before. I feel like it should never occurs as thus, but my options are limited in this situation. Where's Haukter I wonder? Did he not expect me to survive? He would be here at the graveyard. Very curious. My body's completely calm now, completely calm.

When they got to my line, those red old men from long ago, they scooped the coal onto my hands with a big metal spoon. The whole procedure of the falling coals looks unceremoniously ridiculous and tedious. The coals went onto my small palm and instead of pulling away I held them and wrapped my fingers around them. I remember the pain spreading up my fingers into my arm. It didn't bother me at all. When I did this the music stopped and the old men stopped moving.

I have to leave soon. I simply had to stop by the graveyard before the battle. Blue never really liked the graveyard. He hated it in fact. I'm glad he doesn't have to concern himself with it anymore. He hated dragging the bodies here. I wonder how many layers of bodies are beneath me. I mentioned it before, but it still vexes me slightly. I wish I could remember how that day ended long ago, how I came to the forest. Those details are lost in the fury of killing. I remember finding the sword, the crawlspace, the armor. My life fashioned itself around those objects. What choice did I have?

The red in that city, it stands out to me now. Why does it distract my memory? Why do I think of it now? I'll take a few more seconds to stare at the dead shapes and triumphs. They don't make feel anything in particular; I just had to see them. I smile. I can kill Haukter. No more charity. I can kill him. It was just a lucky shot—that's all it was, a lucky shot. Something explodes in the distance. The booming bursts crackles through the air and bounces off the trees.

It makes me sick. Run you fool.

The graveyard's behind me now. I'll reach the river soon. My speed's at top gear. The trees mix together; the black and brown, the needles, all their images flowing and following me. I feel like an Ill, running panicked along the mountains cliffs. The Ills, what will be done about them if I fail? My conversation was less than provocative, but like I said before, I left the man alive. Or should I say beast? They've spent enough time sulking in the shadows of the mountain caves. Their evolution might be on the upswing.

I really don't know what I am talking about.

I'm at the river finally. The city will not be far from here. The sheets of ice from my earlier bout still bounce along the dark river, which reflects the random threads of sunlight. I can see the corpses of the men Blue and I killed. The machines are destroyed and turned over. Some are still steaming in the cold sunlight. I assume they were destroyed even further by the outliers, so they couldn't be taken by some other party.

I admire their future sight.

I leap across the plates easily. They barely move beneath my bounds. I come across the man's spear. Normally,

I have no respect for the dead, no patience. It's disgusting. I'm not sure why I decided to change.

I arrive at the eastern bank of the river where Haukter had hit me. A wide pool of blood sits spattered across the bank and ice plates. Blue's blood, I'm sure of it. There are strips of fur and broken arrows everywhere. They must have pinned him here for quite some time. I slash the plate vertically with his leftover scraps.

It'll sink to the bottom of the river.

That will make his soul happy in some way. I'm past the river blood black water.

The city is not far. I will be there shortly. Sunlight spills over the tops of the Shingles and their random block shapes. More trees pass, more trees and snow, more wind howling.

The city grows closer, and I'm feeling better.

I remember them throwing me from the Shingles. The torches, the spinning snow, the sickness of the grey stone passing me. I remember the pain in my arms, when I hit the snowy rock. It's very hard to remember. I had to focus on the killing. My arms hurt from the fall, but they didn't break, nothing did. My bruises healed in days. The wall and Shingles back then were so big and endless. The crawlspace inside of them was large for my little body.

How did I find it again?

More trees, they never end when you're in a hurry. The cold blisters and scorches at its frosty peak. If I weren't running so hard I'd feel it down to my veins and core. More explosions up ahead, blue light spreads in the sky. So close, everyone there must hold on. I will kill them, rest assured.

I'm coming to where the trees begin to thin and the clearing before the edge of the Shingles. I cannot remember many of whom I've killed except for Haukter, his kind I remember very well. I should've killed you Haukter. I should've killed you. The clearing before the Shingles ends quickly. I stop to stare at them.

The wall has been breached. The Shingles have been smashed down at their ancient roots into crumbled piles of old stone. Not all of them are gone, but massive holes outnumber the slabs of stone. Why so many shots into the wall? The last layer, where I was standing just the other day and witnessed the children, has been completely destroyed. Pile of ageless brick and mortar are everywhere. Their machines did it, their armored walking machines with their pretty energy.

I am through the wall.

So strange not to climb it. So strange not to walk high over it. Something new, and something strange. The grey path through the mountain valley into the Diamond Town curls before me. I will not allow them to hurt anyone, to kill anyone. I will not allow the citizens of the Diamond Town to kill either. None of it may happen. I will not allow it. I cannot feel my lungs. I'm almost there. After them Haukter, I will kill you. This is your fault. You allowed them to breach the wall and Shingles. Still, this is my fault, I allowed Haukter to live.

The city, more snow, more wind, the city—I can see it.

Chapter Eight

The Diamond Town

I wish I could understand what I'm seeing. I cannot even describe it completely, like this image wasn't real and plucked from some faraway dream.

Surreal must be the word, surreal.

The city isn't how I remember it, even in my vaguest memories. The city spreads out beneath the grey walls of the split-mountains. The houses are stern sheets of brick squares, which have curved metal tops for roofs. The metal glows a green and brown, like the trunks of the old trees in the frontier. The houses are stacked ridiculously tight together, barely any spare space glows between them. Holding the buildings together are lumps of pink rock, which stick out randomly and obscenely from the walls. The diamonds— round, fleshy and untouched in their natural state. The houses vary in height and width. Some hovels are as tall as the grandest trees, and other I would have to bow my head to get inside. The light coming from the square windows bleeds a lazy orange. It falls out from the thick-waved glass windows in bleached beams, but gets eaten by the sunlight above.

The light makes it seem peaceful, but I know it's a fabrication. The streets twist and worm every able direction in cobblestone trails. They bend and crawl among the buildings in no discernible order. How odd, it's like there was no reason for the roads whatsoever. There are bridges on the roads which curl across the flowing streams drizzling in from the river. The bloody river from before. White flowers line the water's edge in clusters. They glow against the cold flowing black.

I have never seen flowers like that before. I wonder how they got them.

The scene of the city isn't as blatantly ideal, the people are still being slaughtered. As if irony were a sound, an explosion rocks the air and trembles the houses frames. I am running. A roof falls down on my right as I sprint along. It crinkles a metal din across the tight city walls. People are screaming as I run. I pass two bodies as I cross one of the bridges. Two men sit in a bloody pile. They're wearing thin, shredded clothes and their bodies are full of arrows. Their features are mangled by the stalks of quivering black. They're not soldiers, they're not soldiers. I would love to enjoy the detail of this place; after all, I've been protecting it for so long. I can't waste one minute on meaningful reflection.

It's always endless war.

I imagine the people of the city are retreating towards the mountains behind the city. There are hidden paths in the giants of stone. They can take them into the forest and hide until the outlanders have their fill of wanton destruction.

That's what I would do in this situation.

No living thing muddles around, no living thing. It's somewhat concerning. I hear people screaming; very good, screaming means they're alive and fighting for life. I'm passing row after row of these diamond houses. The footsteps are riddled with bodies, children, men, and women. I hear the crossbows rattling against the mountains behind the city.

The requiem makes me bite my tongue.

I round the cobblestone path up the hill towards the mountains belly. They are running into the mountain to take refugee, to outrun the arrows. The city empties the closer I get to the mountains, it looks like the citizens outran the second cloud of arrows, but most certainly not the first. The mountains are towering up in an even row of grey points and settling clouds. The city becomes small and confined behind me as I run. I'm almost beyond its edge. I remember it being so much bigger.

No much time to stare and wonder, to watch the sunlight soak up those heavy windows.

There's an open space where the city ends and the mountains begin, a narrow valley with a flat and rocky-snow ground. People are running out of houses near me, they mob the streets and run in every direction on these narrow stone paths. Some even jump into the streams floating on pieces of broken wood. I'm knocking the people over as I run. My lungs and legs sting and burst. No, I can't be tired at such a pivotal moment. I'm looking forward to it. I'm looking forward to it.

The stone-etched road has grown too tight and convoluted with survivors. I can knock them aside, but that wastes time. They're so weak in their staggers and sprints. Some are covered in blood. Some have had their thin dark clothing hacked off in long strips. I want to look at them more. I'm curious about the citizens.

Very curious.

I crawl up the side of a particularly tall building, which has a blown out wall of crumbled brick. I need the roof to see what's happening. I won't leap up to the very top of this sheet of metal, which would give away my position. I hang off the roof and balance myself on the side of the building. I look back towards the flowing crowds heading towards the entrance of the city and the Shingles. A man has stopped and is staring at me. He's old and has very dark eyes. He looks at me like I know him.

I don't know him, do I?

I can't see anything from my dangling vantage point. I swing up onto the roof. The world seems too chaotic for the outlanders to notice me. On the roof I notice two more large buildings ahead of me. I leap onto the side of one and scamper up it quickly. I need to pinpoint where the people are fleeing into the mountain once they get by the small valley. I'm sure it's where the mountains first open up in honeycomb dark paths. The outlanders won't find it so easily. The clattering brews even louder, the roaring of the machines and their false limbs.

I will cut them to pieces.

The city stretches behind me, the legendary town which the unknown nations covet for legend and reputation. Snow continues to fall lightly on this midmorning. The city looks beautiful beneath the listless petals, like it should never be touched or disturbed. I need to look at it before I turn my eyes to war. The roofs, slanted and flowing to the cobblestone ground in sharp points. The thick windows and their watchful icicles hanging patiently. The sculptures of men and women, lining the paths and buildings, posing in old histories. Despite the blood and wandered rubble, the city glows against the snow.

I wouldn't mind seeing this place again.

I run to the point of the slanted roof and crouch down on its edge. More snow, more cold. I was right. They drove the citizens across the valley towards the mountains. The encroachers moved too fast though, and cut them off before they could reach the mountains. I was wrong to think the invaders wouldn't make it around to flank the civilians. Clever, they're very clever indeed. The outlanders have formed lines, long lines of brown metal with those hammering crossbows. They aren't firing though, into the wide open space filled with civilians. Forms are slashing and charging the outlanders from behind, from out of the mountains. Thousands of them are rushing out onto the armored lines of troops.

It's the Ills.

The encroachers from the south end of the valley, where the city ends before the open space, have rushed past the civilians towards the melee by the mountain. They'll form themselves into a line and cut down the Ills with their arrows and fire. Smart, very smart. There are so many Ills by the mountain, and so many invaders in the valley—you can barely see the grey plateau beneath their feet. The civilians, who were originally pinned in that valley, rush back inside the city in massive droves. The ground quakes to the thousands of feet running, charging, and sprinting.

I'm ashamed of their panic.

The invaders are about to fire into the Ills. All the invaders have been killed beneath the mountain by the Ills. They were swarmed by the Ill's writhing green bodies and didn't have a chance. I don't really remember what I said to their prince, or king, whatever. It must have been something inspiring? I remember Haukter appearing, and our little skirmish, and then running to the river. I remember smashing his chest with my hilt.

The crossbows suddenly rattle like a bunch of hollow snakes. They jolt me back to reality. The waves of armored Ills are mowed down by the long arrows. The crossbows crackle in unison, their commanders must have them trained to trigger in timed fashion. They weren't this coordinated when they fought me.

The Ills looks ready for war. They're dressed less like savages. They're not covered in their typical tattered black armor, but plated smooth metal like men. Their weapons aren't rusted and worn. Their steel looks silver, sharp, and sterile. It's unfortunate, in their new classy look, that they're dying at an alarming rate.

The angle of the valley allows the arrows full velocity as they strike. The black-red shields of the Ills can't hold back their fury. Still, thousands of Ills run forward from the mountains. More arrows though, more open spots start to form in their ranks. Piles of corpses form.

The invader's arrows are stopping the Ills from advancing towards further into the valley and towards the city. The cold helps the invaders, not a single breath of wind throws their arrows off their mark. I will have to intervene soon, but too much distance separates the Ills from their formations. Even I couldn't survive this swarm of troops. There has to be some sort of break to the battle.

The walking machines have lined up between the firing troops. The same formation as they used at the river when Blue and I tore them apart. I remember already, it's a bloody memory. The machines shutter and drift to the ground—and move with the insidious buzzing sound. The metallic thrumming begins in their curved chest. I can already imagine those luminous bubbles growing in their centers like sculptured fire.

The Ills will be completely wiped out.

For some inexplicable reason, I don't want them to be slaughtered. It's strange having this concern for them.

The machines fire a buzzing barrage of emerald orbs. They make a high-pitched cackling sound after they release their condensed blaze. The cold could be warping their systems within; the factory-fire powering them so intensely could be fading. The spheres fly straight into the Ill's massed ranks. Rocks exploded beneath the sizzling light, sending debris into the Ills and leaving their bodies uneven and obscene. Their black blood clouds the snow. The arrows continue to fly at them. Some of the Ills have closely formed their shields together to repel them. The encroachers fire heavily on these clumps, breaking shields and splitting green skin. Ills have lined behind them, despite the deluge of points, and begun firing arrows back at them with their crude bows.

An arrow flies by my head wistfully. They need to adjust their range. Still, I appreciate their strategy.

The arrows are coming more consistently now. A few of the invaders have fallen down with an arrow to a throat or face. The leverage from the high angle of their arrows allows the points to pierce their armor. Ills charge out as the crossbows start to pause and quiet in the invaders ranks. The machines stay silent and steaming in the cold. The snow falls silently and deliberately.

It's good killing weather.

I see the woman towards the center of the formation. She survived what occurred on the lake with Blue—I'm very impressed. I'm sure Haukter's near the city now. He might be inside the walls in fact. I survived his poison. I shouldn't underestimate him.

It would be foolish.

A screeching sound carves upward from inside the invaders formation. A burst of blue light pillars into the sky in a quick line. The machines are working again, they fire immediately at the Ills coming swarms. Everything along the valley explodes in rock and blue fire. No more watching and planning my next move. No more waiting. The city behind me has gone calm as the Ills and outlanders have killed one another. I must drive the outlanders away from the city, even if I can't kill them all. After they're gone, I will find Haukter and kill him. I breathe hard and unsheathe my sword and grip its long handle. Something far away inside of me, tells me not to kill.

I fall.

I'm on the invaders before they can turn around, before they can even breathe, before they can hear my cutting sword. I cut twelve men down on the backside of their formation. They scream and cry beneath my swings. I don't move as fast running along their edges as I could. I want their backside flank to turn to me, to see what I've just accomplished. They bite. Men fire at me, but I outrun their shots and knock the stragglers away with my sword. Someone yells, it's her, the arrows stop their stream. A few arrows dart towards me from behind. Sharp-shooters no doubt, I knock them away quickly with my sword. I run towards a machine that hasn't turned around to face me. The sharp-shooters follow, peppering the back of the contraption and lancing the man inside. I pull on the machine and tip it over. As we topple, I jam the handle of my sword where the dials and buttons sit glowing. The gears hum with surprise and the heart begins to glow. I jump away quickly. Blue explosions shatter the formation throwing rock and blood everywhere, leaving a red smear across the ground. The formation can't keep their eyes on the Ills.

They've finally turned to me—all their hundreds of eyes are on me.

The Ills are coming. The empty space between the two armies dwindles beneath the glowing sun. A man runs out from the formation and arrows. He dives and swings his broad sword at me. I catch the blade with the gauntlet on my left hand and slit his throat. They've circled around me, the man was a decoy.

Very clever indeed.

I sprint directly into the formation and thick lines of troops. I'm running to the line where the Ills will meet them shortly. Something moves quickly on my left—too fast to be one of the pawns. I know it's her. I sprint faster to the front. I'm slashing left and right, as men rise up and fall down against my sword. I hear her scream following. The front line cannot fail or else the Ill's will overrun them, and they're outnumbered despite the earlier slaughter with arrows. I duck beneath a swinging sword and grab one of the men's crossbows. I smash his face open and watch his blue eyes go different directions.

It distracts me slightly, I sprint again.

I fire the crossbow as I'm running. A dead man falls on me and I pick him up at his ankles and throw him over my shoulder. I hold him in front of me as I dash. His body shutters a wild amount, and becomes intensely heavy. More screams and yells fill the air, along with metal smashes and colliding steel.

The ground starts to tremble below the metal maelstroms. The Ills have collided with the invaders and it's an outright melee.

More screams, smashes, and the sound of metal grinding on uncooperative skin. I've seen my fair share of whirlwind clashing, but never one with this colliding force. I cannot help but feel responsible for the massive battle. I'm unhappy with result of all these colliding monsters on the footsteps of the Diamond Town.

I'm very unhappy.

I sprint to the south side of tempest, where the Ills are fewer in numbers. I have no urge to kill them, but I don't want to instigate one with my presence and break this unspoken peace. The invaders are completely focused on the Ills. The Ills have the advantage in close combat. They have superior physical strength and numbers. The clacking of swords and shields thunders remarkably. The invaders move into brown armored clusters and lock their shields together. It's not use though, the Ills spill over them like a green tide and crush the men to death underneath.

I can hear her screaming over the bloody din. She's on the northern edge of the formation killing Ills left and right with her ridiculous axe. Her howls are high, gurgled, and ear piercing. The blue light from her skin and forced strength glow through the thrashing crowd. She breaks direction and loops out of the melee. She's looking for someone inside the battle. It's not me either. I'm not hard to spot. She dashes back in closer to me, but not aiming for me.

She's going after the commander, the prince, the key to peace.

She cuts her way through in a wild wide swing, cutting down her own troops along with Ills. The machines are firing on the melee, creating clouds of dark blue energy and arrows. The Ills are slaughtering the ground troops rather easily, but the machines fire into the swarms leaving the bodies pulverized and mutilated. I've never really seen anything quite like this before.

I'm watching her cut through the Ills towards the prince. I'm holding up hope that one of the Ills will step into her and evade the simple attack, and then stab her through the chest with one of their short spears. None do though, she's fire on ice. I don't think the invaders expected these types of things to be living in the mountains with this inherent furiousness. The Ills were built to brawl in tunnels and caves; a melee like this is practically second nature to them.

They cannot stop her, a new Ill, even multiple, step in front of her, and all are cleaved into portions with her ridiculous axe. They fall to the ground in green and bloody stumps. Her scream follows them as they topple, aching above the souring cold. She's out of control, completely wild, a human animal. I feel sorry for her in a way. I don't want to kill her. Something in my stomach, not quite sure what, but it's there. I can feel it. I can disable the thick tube of metal running along her spin, which delivers her power to the rest of her body. If I disable it, I should cease these berserker tendencies. She might've been a decent human being before hideous the alteration occurred.

It seems distasteful to engineer someone biologically to be a killer.

More Ills fall. I run. She's becoming more savage the closer she gets to the prince. Her white body glows with the blue fire, and the bandages around her have been ripped and shredded by the battle. I cannot allow her to kill him. If the prince falls under her axe there will be no peace, no armistice, only endless killing and no Ills that walk and speak like men. I must save him; there can be no more killing. If I fall to Haukter, who will protect the Ills and the Diamond Town?

I run.

The Ills are clashing savagely with the encroachers as I run through. The steel mixes with crunching bones into a glorious red cauldron of clashing enemies. Shields fall upon shields, sinew and vein mixing in each strike. I dart so fast they can barely sense me, let alone see me. I'm between two invaders and they fire at me. I leap above the arrows as they skewer each other. In my flip, I count the number of Ills between the berserker woman and the prince. I count ten. No Mohawk topped bodyguards from earlier. They would be able to hold up to her strikes, those were scarred fighters. They must be out commanding the wings, taking down the machines. Some men scream and aim their crossbows in the direction of my dash. I cut their faces off in one vertical swipe. I hear quick and throaty gurgles. I'm running even faster than before. I can see the prince's face through the bloody, twisting masses. His face, his nearly human face, he cannot die. She's in front of him. The axe looks wild and gleaming in the sunlight. She's drenched in blood, making her blond hair black and tangled. The prince has fallen down on his back, but holds his curved sword in front of him. He doesn't look scared. I'm impressed. He won't be able to stop the massive axe head.

I leap. I pray. She's swinging his axe down at him.

She takes her time in the middle of her vertical stroke. She must be relishing the moment. Her animal mind can still be sadistic. I get in-between her axe blade and the prince in a quick black metal blur. I've got both hands on my sword. I kick him back away from me. Some of his grizzled troops run to circle him.

The axe head comes down, and I swing my sword to collide.

The shock of the steel hit knocks everyone away from us, like the white sand upon the black waves. The berserker must be at peak strength. My hands tremble under the pressure of grinding axe, it's impressive. Her face shines pale and fades blue. The energy must be bleeding out of her. Her face glows blue tears. You cannot see a single drop of blood, only the priceless blue. What have they made her into? She's inhuman. Her bloody hair billows angrily in the wind. She's bitten her lip, and a blue glow runs down her pale narrow chin. She's bent over me, pouring all her strength and pressure into the obscene axe.

I imagine only Haukter will be stronger than her.

We cannot stay locked like this much longer. Neither soldier nor Ill interferes. She's panting over the edge of the axe. More inhumanity, more inhumanity. I can't maintain this strength any longer, the pressure pushes beyond comprehension. I swing my left shoulder inside the lock with its steel black point. The point knocks the axe head off balance and I slide my sword out from underneath. The axe heads smashes a small crater into the ground in a blue flourish. I break away from her running full speed. I need to get away from the crowds so I can maneuver my long sword more when countering that axe.

Up close, the axe head has complete dominion.

She follows me faster and more wildly than before. She swings the axe at my shadow, just barely missing my legs. The sun hits us with heavy rays and the valley glints stars with all its fallen steel. This sprint moves the ground fast, pretty soon we'll be at the foot of the mountains and hidden paths.

She's beyond fast, I can't outrun her anymore.

She leaps in the air in a blue trailed bound and slams her axe into me. My sword swings up to counter. I grip it with both hands. Sparks shower and rocks split as we swing. Each strike echoes across the mountain side towards the Ills and encroachers. They have completely stopped fighting to watch us.

I would prefer for them to kill one another than to witness this bout.

This combat's getting tiring. I will not be able to beat her with my normal method of strength and speed. She's more disciplined in this rage. I cannot outfight her physically, she's my equal. I'm still a little weak from Haukter's poison, what a fantastic concoction. More clatter and clashing, and smashing. We break from the mountain edges. She follows me, and swings at my back vertically in a leaping strike. I roll aside and let the rocks absorb the frenzy. I make a quick slash at the gloved white hands wrapped around the massive handle. Her skin splits open around her hands and forearms in even little slits. They almost look graceful against her skin. She's quite a specimen.

I break away running after my quiet victory. She matches my speed and slashes again at my shadow. It seems like it will never end. Her cleaves are so close I can feel the cold bite of the axe head on my feet and neck. It's a lovely game we play, nearly a dance actually. It makes me feel empty-stomached to consider this a dance.

I cannot stop her without resorting to a little trickery. I double my sprint with my dead legs and lead her away from the mountains, and into the field of corpses. There are hundreds of them bleaching red and glowing iron in the sun.

There are so many.

She's quickly after me. It's an impressive dash. I cannot outrun her, the glowing potion she uses flows with too much power. I must trick her. She's behind me again. The little break didn't last long. More swings, I leap backwards over them and finally face her without my back turned. She swings at me again wildly, and I back pedal away from each throat-seeking slash. I run out of space quickly. She swings horizontally at me and I counter. The earth shakes with clouds of rocks. Bodies, armor, and weapons fly outward around her feet. We split after our hands start to fail behind the vibrations. I must match the strength to set the illusion. I can feel the corpses brushing and crunching against my feet. A random falling of snow billows quietly against the chaos. My legs burn heavily, and my arms feel like ash.

My limit's nearly here.

No, I can do more. I have fought more than this, and against sturdier opponents. The wind feels better against my skin; the poison might finally be gone. I pull the fire up in me. I pull the strength up in me. I'm upon her slashing. I'm on the offensive. I miss and slash empty red stone. I follow her slashing up and down. She leaps and blocks my slashes with flat side of the axe. She stabs at me with it and I knock it away. Our duel has brought us back in front of the encroachers. I can feel them behind me. There are hundreds of them, and a dozen machines yet, this isn't over if I win this. The raging booms from our strikes echo to the mountains and back. She's quite the monster, quite the monster.

We break again and start running through the battlefield. I have to end this soon before I get desperate and reckless. I loop around in a wide curve on my left. It'll eventually come back to her for a strike. It'll be face to face, axe against sword. She's a second away from carving me, the trick must work. It must work. My sword sits relaxed in my right hand. We've separated enough in the circle, and she's turned around to face me. The axe head comes slowly towards me, leading her blue-blond charge. It swings slowly towards me, like time was holding it for its own watching greed. I swing down at her vertically at full blast. She swings the axe head horizontally to meet my ageless sword. I release my sword as the weapons collide, and my sword flies into the air in an unceremonious clang. I roll head first below her swing and pick up an Ill's sword from a mangled body.

I have one moment, one moment to wound her.

I'm behind her slender body and white cloak. I can see that weird copper implant coiled along her delicate spine. It crawls up to the base of her bloody skull. Some foreign writing dribbles down it. No time to gawk, she's already starting to turn around with the axe. I slash quickly at her spine with the black and awkward curved sword. The implant severs, and blue energy spills out in thick bursts almost like a pressured liquid.

A horrible scream shocks from her bloody lips.

She throws the axe carelessly to the side. Another hiss and burst of light, I jump even further away. I don't want the captured lightning to blind me. She wrenches around wildly like she was pulled by hidden strings and chains. The jade light's being pulled out of her back by some phantom force. It looks sad. I've never faced encroachers like this before. I breathe in deep and run to the Ills who stand awestruck. I settle down next to the prince breathing heavily. He looks at me surprised and relaxed. I think he wants to say something to me, but doesn't know what.

The encroachers quickly run out to her and scoop her and the axe up. Her bodies gone still, but I think she can still breathe. Steam rises off her frayed form in delicate streams.

Nobody moves. We're all captivated by the moment. It rarely happens to me. The wind howls quietly. A whirring sound fills the air. It's a machine getting ready to fire. The peacefulness was short-lived. The melee starts again like an unshackled storm. Arrows fill the air. A machine walks directly behind us with groaning anger. It's trying to take out the prince, I know it. I grab the whelp and run. Ill's pour onto the glowing machine and skewer the pilot with two spears.

I need my sword. I need it.

Two of the machines rotate towards me and the prince. I need to get him out of here. I run back towards the Diamond Town. They glow beneath their chests and hum two fiery orbs. I duck as the two discs buzz by me and into the homes of the diamond town. Splinters and rocks shatter everywhere. Some of the debris rains on us unceremoniously. Blood drips down my nose and left eye.

It has been a long time since I have tasted my own blood. It tastes good. I smile.

I run into the narrow alleyways of the Diamond Town with the prince. They're filled with cracked rock and halved cobblestones. I crawl up a tall building with him and put him by the dark chimney on the roof. He's completely befuddled by my actions, but he's too scared to say anything. An orb shatters the building beneath our feet. We fall down and I leap onto the other building as the walls crumble.

His survival has become paramount.

I shield the Ill with my body. Arrows flood into the alleyways. The Ills need to storm those machines. I wish I could see what's happening out there. If I were in the invaders position, in a hopeless battle, I would be trying to take out their leaders too. Arrows are now arching up over the rooftops and falling on us. I pull the curved sword out of his trembling hand and knock a few away that dive close. A machine has started walking toward the edge of the city. I can see its blocked shape through the tight buildings. A blue orb blossoms up from the center of the machine. It'll turn us to dust. I can't leap, dodge, or bend. We're completely vulnerable here, since the building behind me has crumbled, and there are too many arrows in the sky. There are screams behind the machine. Four Ills have crawled onto it from behind as the machine roars. One falls in front of the jutting chest and dashed to pieces by the growing fire. The other three pull back on the walking machine and it falls over them.

One gets crushed, but the other two stabs the men to death with curved knifes. I smile at the sight.

The disc still fires at us in a hobbled streak.

Something strong has its arms around my waist. The ground sizzles with rock and fire beneath our gliding feet. We're in the air and on top of the roof in a few bounds. It's one of the bodyguards from earlier with Haukter. His used his monster strength to leap up the narrow walls, grabbing the two of us.

The Ills have saved my life.

The invaders start pouring into the city like wild brown ants. The Ills have won, the men are retreating. They have no more machines to protect them. The last machine was the one those four Ills mutilated. I leave the prince against the crumbled building and watch the men retreat. Only fifty of them left, at the very most.

I'm impressed. I'm happy. I smile wide, and the Ill prince laughs nervously.

The ant invaders are carrying the berserker woman on their shoulders as they scramble. I'm impressed with their stamina after such an amazing battle. I follow them with my eyes as they pick a random alley to run through into the city.

I will pursue them. I will.

The dead cover everywhere, and their splashes of blood stain the snow in elaborate designs—a lovely sight for someone like me. The Ills are weeping human sobs and crying into their hands. It was a terrible battle. Thousands were killed, thousands. The Ill leader behind me coughs and stands up from the shattered roof we're standing on. He's uninjured, tall, and man-like. He looks so young, so much time for everything. He's starting at me as Ills and blood covered townsfolk stagger about. Two men carrying my sword fall on their knees in front of the building and start sobbing. It's very embarrassing. I follow them with my eyes. I cannot show any emotion, none. Ills are walking over in droves. They're covered in blood and peeled green skin. Men, women, and children spill out of the city to help them walk and stagger. Normally, they'd scream and run at their approach.

I must give chase to the invaders, no time for socialization. I wish there was slightly, but no—too much damage has been done. I turn to the Ill prince; he's staring out through the afternoon snow. I stare at him directly in his narrow colorless eyes. He trembles under my blood soaked gazed.

I smile large and show my teeth. I wink, and I fall off the roof. I grab my sword and run.

The streets do not seem as short as they were before, especially absent any explosions or arrows. I want to catch the surviving men and the berserker. I want to catch them, kill them, but save her. I won't kill her. The streets seem so endless, like it all seems so unfamiliar to me even though I just dashed through it a short time ago. One house makes me feel warm as I pass it, like I've been there before. It's a strange sensation. I'm getting closer to the edge of the city and beginning of the Shingles. My legs feel light and enthusiastic. After I kill Haukter, there will be no more fighting.

I can't even imagine what that will be like.

The candles are being relit in the windows along with lanterns in the alleys. The city's coming alive again. It heals me to see it stir, not all life was lost. I can see the wall, and Shingles growing in front of me in their shattered parts. It reminds me, it reminds me of the killing, the protection, my task, my authority. I must run faster so they may die and I can confront Haukter. He could kill all the Ills and the people, easily.

Haukter's truly haunting me, a ghost in the woods.

I'm at the edge of the town. There are people here where the rubble from the invaders first entrance has been built. Hundreds and hundreds of people are mulling around the small bridges and pathways. They're watching me profoundly, like they were looking at a ghoul or specter, like they could see through me. It's very strange. Some people are crying, some clapping, others just watching. An older woman in the crowd gazes at me, something about her eyes, brown and heavy like mine, something twists me inside. She's from somewhere, or something. She's someone in relation to me, she recognizes me. I start to panic and breathe long, I cannot stay here. I push my way through the crowd. I cannot stay here; it's not correct and negligent. I must leave. I must leave. I walk past them all, including her, and jump up to the parted and dissolved roof of a nearby house.

I turn to them slowly, awkwardly, and without looking at one person in particular. I try to watch their eyes, but I panic. I'm going to say something.

"I," I say, but words aren't coming out right. Not that they ever did.

"I'll," I stagger again. Please, I need to speak. You need to say something. Look at the blood and death. You can speak.

"I'll always," I stagger. A woman cries in the huddled crowd. I stand up straight and look at the line of faces with bloody marks.

"I'll always be there, to protect you from the monsters."

I run.

Chapter Nine

The Berserker

They're not far ahead of me. I will meet them soon. I have not thought about the outcome yet; specifically, how I will spare her, and how I will kill Haukter. I really don't have any answers on how I will accomplish these things, I can only theorize, and act on instinct. I'm in the forest now. I've just cleared the outskirts of the walls and Shingles. Those walking-machines the invaders used were maniacal and blind, they caused unmatched damage. I don't know how future guardians will fair against these advancements. If I spare her and she can return, maybe that will cease the invasions. It'll make them realize there's nothing on this island but monsters and shattered men.

She must return to them.

The evening's going to be arriving soon. I hope they can still light the torches for me and my hunt. The battle in the city, which has never occurred in its existence, appeared to last only a few moments, but in reality took the entire afternoon. I will never understand how time passes in combat. Another blood-riddled reason my memory and life lives like a blur. I'm tired on the inside.

I will not show it, but I am.

The poison, Blue, the Diamond Town, it has all been exhausting. Blue was more deserving of shallow grave though,

I had to do it right, I had to dig it deep. He had value. He had love.

The evening beams will be heavy and diluted by the cold tempests. I imagine it looks quite nice on the white sand and black water on the shore. I hope to see it again someday. I'm running between the trees; they're quiet, solemn, and awaiting the night. They look so permanent, so sturdy, it's hard to believe anything could topple them, but our axes do it all the time.

At least they grow back.

I must concentrate. I cannot be distracted. The chances of me making a mistake are growing exponentially. After the encroachers there is only Haukter. I have absolutely no idea how I will deal with him. The thought of not having confidence hurts more than the doubt. I'm not comfortable, or used to this feeling.

I'm almost to the river. They'll be crossing it—the same watery spine as before, with its frosty marks of blood. They'll still be there. I don't want to see them. Maybe some of the cold and snow will smear away the marks. The snow has been so peaceful recently though, unlike the cold, an invisible blister. All this combat and strife, and the snow still twinkles in uncensored petals.

The natural world isn't without a sense of humor.

The trees are thinning ahead, the river will be near. I can hear them panting and running on the plates of ice. They are panicked; they know I'm on their trail and not the Ills who are too decimated. The Ills don't pose a threat to anything or anyone. They've outgrown their bloodlust and their violence. That means something to me, I don't really know what, but I can feel it behind my eyes. The wound on the top of my head from the shrapnel has dried. It feels strange to have the air parting the skin, the biting coolness where the tissue has been split. The pain feels illuminating. It has been so long since I've felt it.

I appreciate its splendor, its reality.

The trees are thinning even more rapidly. I know they're not far. I'm curious to see their state. I break through the edge and the open land splits between the river and woods. The plates are moving towards the center of the dark line.

It's them.

Fifty left, just fifty of the invading force. They're staggering and trembling as they run. Their brown armor has been shredded and covered with slight crystals of frost. They have glistening wounds as well, but they keep running for the shore. I have to give them credit for running in that state. She's running also, apparently my wound was painful at the time but not debilitating. Something moves on the opposite side of the shore. A form lunges out from the trees and onto the plates.

It's Haukter.

He's moving fast, at a full hide-covered sprint. I can't even see his feet touch the ground beneath the animal layers. They see him immediately. He's a bit of an eye sore. I would hope they'd see him. I stop quickly and sink back into the thin trees. I'll leap into the fray, but I'll have to play it just right.

Haukter has a weapon at his left side, the big axe-head cleaver from before with the strange handle. They fire arrows at him from their crossbows. His right sleeve flails up and knocks them away leisurely and violently. A strange combination of skill and rage. I won't run yet. I have to surprise him. I have to take out one of his eyes to handicap him. I need the advantage. I'm too exhausted.

He releases the clever at them. It's attached to some sort of chain with small brown handle added for stability. The cleaver makes a light humming sound as it spins towards them. They must be panicked. They're running into a clump and not spreading out. The blade hits them spinning. A few duck, but the rest are cut in half at the waste.

Quite the weapon, I'll have to hurry.

Haukter retracts the cleaver back to him with a pull of his left sleeve. The range of the attack gives the invaders a few moments to recover. She charges Haukter totally normal, and not controlled by rage. Her axe dangles out at him as she closes the distance. Haukter recoils the weapon in a quick snap and holds it in front of his body. The remaining men skillfully fire arrows at him around her charging form. He knocks them away again with his right sleeve, not that they could pierce his hides. He brown rod falls out of his right baggy sleeve. He swings the rod and cloud of red darts with white feathers breaks the air. She ducks, but the men behind her fall to the ground convulsing wildly and thrashing. Soon they'll be dead.

They're all taken down except for her. She is the only one left. She is the only one left.

I run. I'll have to jump at him for leverage. I admit— I'm a bit intimidated by Haukter. I break from the forest and the hill overlooking the river. He doesn't see me sprinting. I think, humorously enough, he's captivated by the woman. Haukter must surely remember them? She sprints close to him. She'll be no match for him, especially without her drugs and extensions. She swings the ridiculous axe nonetheless and smashes it into his blade. He's a little surprised by her strength. I can tell he braces himself a little with his cloaked legs. Haukter still shrugs her off of him and she falls to the ground panting. I wish I knew what he was thinking. My sword's out, I'm a few steps away.

The moment I'm in-between them, I slash at his hood towards his right eye. I can't miss. I can't. This will be my only chance. He's surprised by my appearance and wrenches back from me swinging his cleaver wildly. I must've hit him, he's disoriented and wild. Blood dribbles against the air. He leaps even further back away from me, kneeling down with a sleeve over his eyes. I grab the woman and her axe. She's in shock. She feels light and soft. I have her beneath my arm. Haukter's screaming in a low gurgle, like a burned beast. How dramatic. I run full speed away from his trembling form. I wouldn't be able to contend with him and his rage.

I run. I run. I run and I don't look back into the woods.

She's heavy beneath my arm as I run, or at least more than I expected. She's the first woman I've touched. Pretty pathetic at my age, but it never seemed like it was part of my role, and like I said never raped women. I'm not a monster. We're in the forest now and I'm still running full speed. I need to give us some distance. He won't be slowed by his eye for long. It seems somewhat cheap to have taken out his eye so unexpectedly, but he did hit me with a dart on the river edge.

It's fair in logic, but not in morals, do those two ever coincide?

Trees are thickening up in walled rows of trunks and needles. We're getting closer to the graveyard. That'll be the place for me to make my stand, a fitting spot for my showdown with Haukter. How exciting, my chest is filled with an eerie brew of anticipation.

We'll battle above all the old invasions, machines, routines, murders, frosts and snows.

We're here, next to a cluster of old rolling machines, which look like long boats on wheels. I set her down next to the rusty juggernaut, which stands twice as high as me. It's covered in a soft green moss with a skeleton encrusted in black dirt hanging out from a square window. It's near the center of the graveyard, away from the piles of frost covered bodies. The snow falls lightly. The cold feels frigid, but distant, some faraway nightmare. The sky has a thin layer of grey clouds. The evening sun will be green and faded behind the winter sky.

She's wrapped her semi-white cloak around her. She's completely covered in blood and patched dirt. She's staring at me with those sapphire eyes. I want to speak to her. I know she speaks my language. The man with the spear professed it earlier. I cannot prevent my body language from looking stiff and knowingly awkward.

"Aren't you going to kill me?" she says sharply in a quiet voice.

The snow falls quietly, there is literally no point to her to maintain some sort of identity.

"There is no point to kill you, there has been enough killing," I say in my most gentle voice. I feel like she's a precious deer I could scare away with the smallest footstep.

She stands up gingerly and scans the tops of trees. I can hear the shore in the background bashing. She looks around the graveyard with withering eyes.

"You did all this? You killed all these people?" she asks.

I stare at her. I'm surprised by her honesty.

"No, not all, some were here before at the bottom of the piles. I added to it." I reply.

"That's hideous," she says.

I don't say anything. She starts to walk around more. I relax a little.

"So, who are you?" she asks.

I'm a little surprised by this question.

"The man who walks the woods," I say quietly.

More snow, more waves rolling far away.

She laughs slightly to herself and wipes some of the blood off her face with her gloves. Her pale skin looks soft and elegant.

"And what is that?" she asks.

I answer quickly to not be embarrassed.

"The Guardian, the one protecting the city and the island from all encroachers and invaders."

She looks at me and smiles blood.

"Of course, I already knew that," she laughs.

"I would imagine so," I reply quietly.

"I know a lot about this island. Years back we sent a few invasions here to scout it. We invested a lot in knowing. It's quite a thing, this island." She says.

"It is," I reply.

She begins to cry in soft, jeweled tears. She leans back down against the rusted machine. I continue to watch her.

"So what are you going to do with me if you won't kill me?" she says quietly through a shackled sob.

"I want you to leave," I say quickly. She stares at me.

"I want you to tell whoever sent you there is nothing here, but monsters and killers. There is no treasure, no magic, no sacred city, just timeless devils."

She stares at me some more. She's confused by me.

"You'd think someone who has been physically altered to become a war weapon would have some incentive," I say sharply.

She laughs at this through some narrow tears.

"Incentive? They, Kain, gave me no choice, only my veins would work for this," she points at her spine.

"These extensions," she whispers.

She gets up again and paces in the light snow. No faraway signs of Haukter yet.

"What about you? Don't you have incentive to stop, you have something else in your life besides this glory," she snarls waving her hands.

"No, the only thing that loved me is dead. You encroachers killed him. The city has been attacked. I see no value in anything anymore."

"No value in anything?" she says.

"Blue's dead, the city's been shattered, these moments were written long ago when I was thrown from the wall," I say.

"How can you not be impressed with what you've done? One man killing thousands of people? Do you not look at it like that?" She says.

I look around timidly. I see no absolute glory in what I've done.

"Is there more than one of you? Who is the man covered in the hides, skulls, and antlers? Is he your partner?" She asks.

"No, he most certainly is not," I snap.

She looks surprised, even mildly scared, but interested.

"Then who is he? Why was he attacking us? This place makes no sense whatsoever." She says.

I get angry at this response, but there's no point to my anger. I'm at a stage where very few vanities matter.

"He is a mistake?" I say quietly.

She continues to look surprised.

"A son?"

I feel somewhat revolted.

"No, a mistake, an exception, an error from a long time ago," I say.

She looks at me rather annoyed. More quiet snow.

"Can you be a little more specific?"

Her knowing that I won't kill her has made her bold. It should.

"He was with a group of invaders who came here some time ago. He was a child then, and I spared him."

"I understand," she says.

"You do?"

She stays somber.

"At least you have prevented yourself from killing the young, killing the children, I couldn't even manage that, all I could see was the emerald fire everywhere."

I believe her. I believe her.

"Yes, well, I have killed thousands of small Ills, which are comparable to people, and," I stop slightly when she looks at me.

"So don't worry, I'm miserable also, at least you had no control."

I lean on the machine next to her and look out into the woods. I'm getting nervous.

"What will you do now about him? You nearly killed him earlier," she says.

"I will kill him," I answer quickly.

"You said no more killing earlier. Do I need to be afraid?" She says.

"He's the last one, it will end with him. I will finish what I've started. Besides, there is no one who is match for him besides me," I say.

"William, the man with the spear you killed, you're very similar to him," she softly says.

"Then he must've been very miserable also," I stammer out.

"I think everyone must be," she says.

Silence drifts in with the quiet snow and green evening light.

"What will you do after you kill him, can you just stop this way of life?" she asks.

"I will throw myself into the black water on the shore where the white monsters are, and I will die."

She looks at me startled and almost afraid. It has been so long since I have seen such outright human emotion besides fear and death. She smiles.

"No more killing?" she says smugly.

I smirk to myself and walk away from the toppled machine.

"That only ensures it, besides, I don't deserve to live or die in the presences of others. I deserve to die alone."

She just stares at me and says nothing. I have worn out my dialogue. We did pretty well for having been enemies the last four days. The snow starts to fall harder as the wind whirls upwards. He's coming. I know it. The natural world knows what lies ahead. I turn to her. I will run out to meet him, the monster, the demon, the lurking cannibal.

"I suggest you hide or be hidden. He will kill you and eat you if I die, but I won't let that happen. Don't worry; I won't let you be killed."

She looks pale, beautiful, a weapon of war disabled. I stare at her. My eyes get lost on her lines, and her matted hair.

"What's your name?" she asks with a pair of wide eyes.

I smile, and I run.

Chapter Ten

The Shore

The snow is falling harder now, much harder, like it wants us to stop and remember the higher forces above our feuds. The forest looks bright and flourishing as I charge into it. It's beautiful and endless. I could watch and witness it every day, knowing the end was near.

I'm running out to him.

I cannot meet him in direct combat right away. He has too many weapons, too many secrets. My physicality will not be able to compensate for it entirely. Most of the weapons Haukter has hidden were designed to kill or counter me, which makes me very uncomfortable. I'm excited also; however, no negative thoughts.

I will kill him. I will kill him.

I'm far enough away from the graveyard now. I'm closer to the shore. My only hope and strategy is to wear out his weapons and draw him into the graveyard. There, I'll be able to use the obstacles and shapes to slow down his attacks. I will need all the help I can get, which I'm embarrassed to admit. The heavy cleaver on the chain will be the most dangerous. I will have to counter it immediately, and it'll probably sap my strength.

I stop running and look out into the forest. The snow has gone silent in its glides, nothing but a random occurrence from the muddled flurries.

Perhaps the world's living and omnipresent eye happens to be fixed on Haukter and I, and the flurries follow it's every blink. The winter, the island itself, brewing some wild storm for us to slash and dice in.

I hear running, it's heavy and concrete. It's Haukter. He's coming with all the vengeance and hate of anyone or anything I've ever killed. The beast has come to pay homage to the monster that made him.

I'm running into the woods towards the sound of breaking trees. I break sideways to him so he notices me. I can see his massive shape through the trees and needles. Running sideways into a battle, what a beautiful and strenuous dance. The trees shutter and spill snow as we brush against them. The sprint covers hills and broken trees. We cover a ton of space. We're both equally fast and darting.

I have a hidden trick with me, which Haukter will not expect. My sword's drawn in my right hand. I keep the long, narrow blade pointed down as I run. It's for balance, and style. In my left hand, slightly concealed by the rushing trees, happens to be the berserker's battle axe. I have borrowed it to surprise Haukter. He won't expect it. My sword shimmers in the evening light. I know his one eye focuses only at its narrow blade. I keep it close to conceal him from it. No doubt he's studying me in the rushing woods.

I hear a humming sound drown out the crackling wood beneath our feet. Haukter's body suddenly thrashes and twists beneath his skulls, feathers, and antlers. The heavy blue-steel of the cleaver curves towards me like curled lighting. It cuts down trees in heavy beautiful bursts. I barely leap above the spin of the signing blade. Some trees topple down behind me. Their groans are deafening as they stagger earthward. I fall back into them as they lean and tip. He follows and sends the cleaver after me with a twist of the chain. I didn't want to use it this early into combat. I run up the falling trees leaning diagonally. Haukter runs directly below me swinging the cleaver. The chain gives it too much momentum. I have no choice. I have to use the axe. It's behind my back. He throws the cleaver directly at me in a vertical spin. I have no choice. I swing down with the axe in vertical smash. The heavy cleaver and axe collide in a sparking cloud. It rattles my shoulders and hands, and knocks me even higher into the pillowed eves. It's the hardest collision I have ever had. The cleaver rolls back to Haukter who leaps out of the way.

Snow and dirt flies, trees fall. The metal smash still echoes across the trees.

I land quickly among their eaves and ride them back to the white ground. I run at full speed into the forest. I must wrap the chain around all the trees and sever it with an axe. I dart randomly between the trees. He's behind me already and running up fast. He knows at a closer range he won't need to extend the chain to try and hit me. The less amount of chain, the more dangerous it'll be for me. I increase my speed through the trees. He throws the blade behind me in a horizontal glimmer. It hums and whines. Snow falls in front of me. I leap at just the right moment and two tall trees fall severed in front of me.

I run back towards him as he pulls the blade back to him. He twists the chain just right so the cleaver follows me. I duck beneath the spinning metal. Haukter twists himself to avoid the direct force of his own cleaver. His left sleeve swings up quickly and a gnarled wooden claw emerges catching the blade. A few of the points crack off under the heavy metal, but it maintains. He caught the blade himself, he must've been practicing. His sleeves quiver beneath the weight of the blade. He snaps his body in a fur-filled twist and throws the blade at me. I'm too close to knock it away. I'll have to bring the combat close to him. I leap in the air and arch my back. I slam into the blade with both hands wrapped around my axe. The cleaver falls back into Haukter who gets crushed against a few trees by my falling weight. The cleaver glows a steel-poison bleached blue. Dried blood has crusted itself around the rippled edge. I look into the slit of beaming skin and eyes atop the mass of fur. Just one blue eye glows back at me. The other has been bandaged with feathers and mud. He throws me off of him with a quick push.

He's strong, and full of blood-craving youth.

I swing my sword at him with my right hand the moment we break. His claw snaps out to block it. I kick him in the chest, twisting my body with my foot and throwing him into a few trees. My boot thumps steel as it collides with the bubbled hides.

I run sideways again. He follows, but not fast to overtake me. He's a little intimidated, the kick probably stunned him. He throws the cleaver again at me with a metallic sideways arc. What marksmanship he has developed with it. I wedge myself against a tree to absorb the force and prevent being knocked off my feet. I turn with the heavy axe and strike it again, and another blue-steel collision. The cleaver ricochets back at him and I follow its spinning song. He leaps back from the blade as it spins. He doesn't have enough time to counter both of us in. I slash him with my sword straight through the chest. A layer of fur drops off revealing another row of tanned hide and feathers.

I will take off all your layers Haukter.

Haukter plucks the blade out of the air and leaps backwards between the trees. I drop my sword and grip the axe in both hands with all my strength. There is another collision between axe and cleaver, monster and man. Trees fall, the ground parts beneath our feet, and snow flies up and down in every direction. We break from the collision immediately; neither of us wants to be locked together.

He stares at me as we run. He's impressed, I know it.

I run for my sword and grab it wildly with my shivering hand. The vibrations are still tickling my bones. I turn back to his flowing form and throw the axe at him in a crooked sideways spin. I know it won't hit him, but I want him to become comfortable with my limitations, that way he might make a mistake. He ducks and twists against the massive axe head. The axe brushes against him. He couldn't move because he's too busy maneuvering the cleaver. He sheds another hide and the axe spins through the empty air into a tree which falls into two chunks. I run again, and he swings the chain and guides the blade to meet me. The cleaver throw was a desperate fling. He's underestimating my change in direction. He clearly expected to be more on the offensive with this battle. I sprint in random dashes and twists. The blade follows me, like an edged animal sniffing the air. I dash left and right around sturdy trees, which can handle the weight of the chain.

Whatever direction I break, the blade follows and strains against the trees. I can hear the wood squeaking and thrashing behind me. A massive grey tree sits in front of me. I make a sharp turn to my left and come around it. I can feel the cleavers massive shadow on my snowy tracks. It clangs around the tree, hooked and stuck in its massive trunk. I stare back at the chain as I break the corner, its taunt like rolled wired. I have one moment to do this, one moment. I hear running, and the chain slightly goes slack. Haukter realizes his mistake. No matter though, I swing with my sword in both hands at the massive chain and it comes apart in a clean serrated edge snap. The massive cleaver falls to the ground with a boom of distant thunder. One less obstacle for me, and one more for Haukter to overcome.

I run for the graveyard.

To my surprise Haukter gets creative and swings the chain at me the moment I begin to run away from the severed cleaver. He might've expected my victory against the cleaver. The chain reaches me quickly in a wild thrash. I manage to get my sword up the moment the snake hits. The collision sends me crashing into a cluster of trees. My ribs get crushed, something pulls in my back, and the light brightens in the eaves. I'm on my feet quickly from the pile of down trees. He's running straight at me, the behemoth of dead skin and fur. He reaches behind his shoulder and grabs the strange bundle of branches. I've always thought it was firewood he brought along to his every location. He's holding the tied up pile with his right hand. It's a weapon, how exciting.

He throws the brambly bundle at me. I leap away quickly to my left keeping my eyes on the hidden weapon. I have little or no idea what to expect. Something in my gut told me not to duck. How fortunate I didn't, since the bundle isn't just some muddled mass but a narrow sheet of thorny branches bound together. No doubt it's covered in poison. If I had doubted my instinct, I would have been crushed by the strip of pointed wood. Haukter swings the sheet at me with both his sleeves. It can be easily manipulated like a flowing piece of cloth. I leap into the air spinning away from its increased range. It follows me like a spiked tongue into the tree-filled air. The sheet doesn't have the best range, but the sea of evaporated poison on it makes up for its limitations.

I'm impressed with all of Haukter's hidden weapons so far.

I run away from him to plan a strategy. He follows contorting the poison thorn ribbon. The entire weapon has been covered with narrow round thorns. I need to make a point on the weapon I can leap off and slash it in two. I slow down my run and let the strand catch up to me. He swings it sideways at me trying to catch me between the narrow trees. I slash backwards at the strip taking a few points off. Not enough yet. Not nearly enough. I swing again, but he twists the ribbon so my sword gets caught in the hundreds of branches. I lose my leverage and my sword, and I'm knocked to the ground. He pulls the weapon up, and slams the sheet down toward me. I roll away backwards before it hits me, with the points just missing my back and hair. I'm faster than he can manipulate it. I'm on my feet and running away from him weaponless. He contorts the ribbon so it clamps and hugs the trees behind me. I double back and wrench my sword free of the poisoned mass.

He screams in frustration. An animal howl.

I slash again, at the beginning of it. More thorns fly off unceremoniously. He swings the band at me again. I jump off the tree with my left foot and over the spiked horror. He's got to be frustrated by my speed.

Didn't he expect me to fight?

I fall to the uneven white ground from my flip, and break away running. He follows swinging and contorting the ribbon, and each time I slash at its stretched front end. He's following me so routinely for the basic effort to judge me, to understand what I'm trying to do in this combat. If I could've given him advice, I would have told him not use such a bulky weapon. I continue to slash at the ribbons head until it's completely clear of the thrashing points. I'm faster than him and break towards the graveyard. I'll need to pick my moment just right, the exactly perfect moment.

He's more inexperienced than I thought he'd be. I'm disappointed.

I give myself some space as he chases after me with the whipping bundle of poison. I stop abruptly, and leap back at him. He brings the ribbon up towards me. I bounce off the flat end of the branches. He waves the band up to me, but the hump doesn't hit me, I'm too close to him. I slash down hard into the beginning of his poisonous sheet. The ribbon falls to the ground unraveled in a disheveled wooden string. He swings the remnants up at me. I twist my body and knock them away with my sword.

Very close, that was very close.

I fall to the ground and I have to defend myself immediately. The tube with the darts from the river where he killed all those men, it's out of his left sleeve. I knock it away from me as swings around to use it. He smashes into my chest with his other sleeve and I fly backwards. He swings the pole at me, throwing the red tipped darts everywhere. I'm above them quickly in a forward jump. He swings the rod at me releasing more darts. I slash them away and knock a few back at him. His sleeves twirl around loosely knocking them aside. It was a good trick Haukter, but not good enough.

I run.

I'm in the graveyard now, or the very outskirts of it. I'm confident I have eliminated most of his weapons to use against me. Brute strength will be next, I know it. I know how this works, he doesn't. He's following me into the graveyard. He fires more darts at me with the slashing rod. I knock them away casually, barely looking back. Another rod emerges from his right sleeve and an even larger cloud follows me. I sprint faster and slash a few small trees down to knock the cloud away. They oblige with aching falls and tumbles. The destruction to the forest in this combat can only be described as monumental. I pick up speed and break away from him. He follows.

I'm waiting for him at a small clearing, marked by a pile of frosted and mossed corpses. Behind me sits a toppled walking machine, which was shredded and dismantled long

217

ago. I'm standing perfectly still. My sword's dangling in front of my feet. He emerges from the trees like a faceless beast, walking slowly and quietly. He's acting more confident, and standing straighter. He knows he has the advantage because of his youth and size. He walks over to me slowly, he's panting in long streams.

So am I.

I haven't fought like that for a while, where not a hint of error is allowed. Haukter reaches behind his left shoulder into his back. I take a stance pointing my blade diagonally at his hulking form. I see his hand for the first time as he reaches. It's white and callused. It glows against his dark brown hides.

Haukter reaches into an opening in one of his hides and pulls something out slowly. He's watching me methodically. It's a spear, a huge spear, nearly twice as long as me. It has a metal point on the end of it, but it's rounded, and sharp. Where the metal connects to the staff, a jagged rocky shape shields the base of the point. Almost like a mud had been wrapped around it in a clumsy point. The staff looks fire-hardened black. He probably burned it for days in a controlled forge. Quite a weapon and he kept it completely concealed. I'm not even sure how that's possible.

He grips the spear in both hands and sprints at me through the peaceful falling snow.

The point comes at me quickly. I knock it away and slash at him in fast rising arcs. The point of the spear doesn't counter my slashes though. Instead his left hand breaks from the handle and that mangle curved claw dangles out. He's fighting me with two weapons, what an enemy.

We break from our quick melee and run sideways back into the trees. He's stabbing at me quickly, and I deflect each stab with my sword. He slashes at me with his claw, but I duck and twist my body keeping my sword free for the spear. I leap at him slashing down and taking away the short advantage of the claw. The claw flies up at me on a hidden chain. I knock it away with my sword, but not before the handle of his lance slams into my stomach. I grab the handle as I spit blood and wrench the spear away from him in an armored twist. He swings the claw around at me and throws some darts with his free sleeve. I throw the spear into him. He ducks and sheds another one of his hides. I leap away, keeping my face to him. He can't have many hides left, it's not physically possible.

He grabs his spear and chases me.

I'm coughing and spitting blood as I run. Something was broken when the lance jabbed into me. He leaps at me and ends the distance between us. He throws both his spear and claw at me in a whirling, stabbing maelstrom. Darts follow like little children. I'm swarmed with them. I spin around a tree and the spear and claw miss. The darts I knock away with my sword panting.

Anymore? Are there anymore?

Haukter stops and slowly pulls a weapon out of his right shoulder. It's a huge, curled blade like the one he had chained for throwing. It can only be described as a cleaver, a butcher cleaver. It's smaller than the chained one, and it has a small black handle at its curved base. Two more rods drop out of the sleeves, the long wooden ones with hundreds of holes for the darts to fly though. They're empty and obsolete. Is he telling me that's it, no more hidden weapons? How irritating, I won't believe him, how many combinations does he possibly have? How many tricks does he possibly have?

This is the little boy I spared so long, this monster who devours men. I didn't know he'd alter and corrupt. I only knew somewhere inside of me it was wrong to kill a child, even if it meant my own death. Blue, why did you have to die? Blue would've lived longer than me. Untaro's live twice as long as any man. He would've been able to help me with Haukter. Now, I'm alone with this monster.

I run.

He matches my speed easily and swings at me. He's fast with the cleaver. My blade, thin and needle-like, jabs and swings at him in our sprint. Each time the clever easily matches my attack. If he swings too wide, I can sneak a few slashes at his hides, but his sleeve whirls around to knock my blade away. His attacks are violent and powerful, he knows he has the upper hand in this brutish battle. I need both hands to repel his slashes, both hands to stop the oblong, yet curved point from ripping me open.

We dash to a group of old man-like machines sitting idle in a large frost covered circle. I leap into the structures of old machines and bodies. He follows, and I jump backwards watching his swings, and parrying the ones getting too close. My arms are slowly tearing and breaking, they feel like limp fire.

The machines are all around us now, giants watching us nearly. He's stabbing with the cleaver now, and it's getting harder for me to knock the blade away. I leap between two machines and the cleaver hacks and split them. I guess it was only a temporary wall. The power of pure rage, I can't contend with it in my withered state. I must sacrifice a part of myself to hit him, make him focus on the pain, and not the approaching goal.

He's trying to lock our weapons up as we parry. He knows he can knock me off balance with his sleeve and then decapitate me. He's swinging wildly as I leap backwards. He stabs and swings. My back bashes up against one of the towering machines. I cannot leap backward any further. He's coming at me. I keep my right arm relaxed with my sword. His sleeve stays motionless. It must look like suicide to him. His dark eyebrows jump as he swings downward at me.

I'm a good actor.

I catch the cleaver in my gauntlet on my left arm. My arm snaps loudly, and immediately breaks without any muscular hesitation. I bite my lip in pain. The blue edge of the cleaver barely bites into arm. I can feel the skin part enough to loosen the tendons and veins. As this happens, I slowly stab my narrow sword through his right shoulder, the sleeved shoulder. He thrashes before it hits, which I expected, and exposes his armpit. The hides are cut to be thinner there and less protective. The point pierces through the thinner hides and upwards through his shoulder. He screams deeply and angrily in a muffled cry. He's not use to pain. The howl echoes into the graveyard wild and feral.

He's very inexperienced with pain.

I'm a little surprised by his reaction. He isn't a fighter like me, but a killer. He's stunned by my sword point. I kick him in the stomach, sending him into one of the machines. It rattles an ancient groan back at him. He jumps back immediately and slashes at me with his cleaver wildly. I counter each slash and our blades ring in the snowy forest. My left arm throbs in pain. His strength's still greater than mine, even one-handed. He's fueled by a twenty-year rage. There is no reason to clash in blind attacks.

Sitting here like ogres hacking at one another, it's hilarious.

I see her now, the berserker, watching us from between a few machines. If Haukter sees her, I will not be able to stop him from killing her. I redouble my slashes against him, putting him slightly on the defensive. My blade becomes liquid and wild. He's just as fast and our blades spark toothy bits in the soft falling snow. I can barely stand as we parry. The battles of yesterday and today have worn me out. My sword cannot take much more either. Without my left arm to stabilize some of the force on the blade, the sword won't be able to absorb the shock of the cleaver. It'll break at any moment. I can feel it in my wrist. I need him to slash up at me in the air. That way I can slash downwards and break the sword.

It might give me an opening.

I leap backwards onto one of the rusted over machines. I stare at him for one heavy-breathed moment, and jump off it swinging down at him with my long blade. I swing the sword like everyone else did before, like I have for everyone, for the island, for Blue, and all the Ills. The cleaver rises up in a horizontal swing. Something sharp trickles behind it, in Haukter's endless sleeve. That's not a surprise. My blade falls onto it and shatters in steely splinters, just like I knew it would. The momentum brings me past the cleaver and onto the ground. The cleaver sails through the broken sword shards and empty air. I watch his one innocent eye staring at me.

The innocent little boy eyes from so long ago, hiding by the trembling firelight in his families tent.

He knows. He knows he's going to die.

I stab the broken sword between the slit surrounding his eyes. The jagged point goes in hard, then soft between his eyes. Haukter gurgles and falls down with a string of blood dripping out of his forehead. I push away his cleaver slowly with my left foot as his body starts to fall away from me. I hold him carefully to me, and slowly put him on the ground. No fighter, no soldier, barely a killer.

There is something in my stomach.

I can feel the opening, a coolness spreading into my chest. I have been stabbed, a dagger, rusty and covered with poison. It belonged to them, his people from long ago. He must've dug it up here in the graveyard one day. I fall to one knee. The poison's working already. I need to leave here.

Of all places, I can't die here.

She's running over to me. She's safe. She stops to look at Haukter and then back at me. She reaches for his hood, and mangled fur.

"Don't touch him," I manage. It'll be hard to speak.

She looks at me with a strange mixture of awe and surprise.

"I don't want to know how he looks," I gasp.

More snow falling, the wind whirls quiet. She steps away from him and approaches me. I can hear the waves, I swear it.

"Please, please, help me get to the shore," I ask. I don't think I'll be able to talk anymore.

I lean on her as we walk. She's strong and gentle with each shaky foot. I use every bit of strength to keep the blackness of the poison away. She's walking and pulling me as fast as she can.

Soon we're on the hills next to the shore. Our walk through the forest was a blur, a blood induced haze. I have lost my concept of time.

But I can still hear the lovely roaring.

She walks me to the edge of the forest where the ground slants down onto the white sand. She stops there, staring at the lapping black waves. She helps me sit down against a tree above the sand. Snow falls on us as we rest against its grey trunk. The evening sun has started to vanish above the grey lines of sea-clouds.

"Bring me to the water please?" I ask feebly. It's rather embarrassing, my weakness. I'm not in the position for vanity. I will never again be in the position for vanity. She kneels down beside me and takes the black glove off my right hand. There's blood on it, it's soaked through. She holds my hand with a gentle, trembling softness. The invaders long ships bob on the black water like long memories. She looks out at the shore and dark sea with dreaming eyes.

"No, you can't get your way," she says. She smiles behind her lips. I hope she can return safely.

I smile—truthfully, and happily. I didn't expect this kindness of not being alone. More blood-haze and faraway thoughts fill my inner eyes. Memories of dying faces, the Shingles, and those tortured Ills brush by me like phantoms. My heart feels heavy for them, and my mind can't focus on anything in particular, just all matters of past and present. I think of myself, and all my actions, and it's as if two minds were within me; the one killing in the open and the other deep within me hoping and praying—I would change. After all, what else separates me from those mindless monsters singing in the deep, but the capacity for change? Snow is falling. The waves roll back and forth against the sand endlessly.

The water looks so cold, so black, and so limitless.